Copyright 2012
Publisher: R. E. Stowell
Fairbanks, Alaska

I can do all things through Christ who strengthens me.
Philippians 4:13

He said to them, "But now if you have a purse, take it, and also a
bag; and if you don't have a sword, sell your cloak and buy one."
Luke 22:36

Cover photo by Rosalyn Stowell
Photo of the author by Samantha Stowell
Thanks for reading it for me, Michelle T. Boyle
Also for being willing to listen & suggest
Thanks to Kara Stowell for proof reading,
Any remaining mistakes are my own.

This is a work of fiction.   Names, characters, places and
incidents are either the product of the author's imagination or
are used fictitiously and any resemblance to any actual person,
living or dead, business establishments, events or locales is
entirely as   a part of the fictional story.   If you recognize
yourself in these pages, you have a vivid imagination and should
be writing novels, yourself.

The Beginning
An Alaskan PAW Novel
Book 1

Chapter 1

It was a dark and stormy night, well, actually, it was a bright sunny day. But it felt like a dark and stormy night. The day had started without any sign of the mess to follow. However, I should have known as soon as I burnt the biscuits at breakfast time that I was not going to have a nice day.

The bear wandered into the yard as I scraped the char from the least burned biscuits and I cut my hand on the knife. I know, don't run away from a bear, it kicks in the charging instinct and besides, I didn't really run. I backed up in a hurry to the porch, stumbled over the stick of firewood I had dropped earlier, sprawled up the steps and skittered on up them and through the door into the house.

So, technically, I didn't run. However, the bear did. I must have scared it half to death with all my backing away and the smell of blood from my cut hand didn't act as an enticement either.

Maybe it was the conversation I was having, too. The bear probably never heard an almost middle-aged woman ranting to herself about the way the neighborhood was going to pot and using a large serrated knife to accent the conversation with scraping sounds and an occasional yelp as I missed the biscuit.

Now people were moving in a couple of miles down the road. That would make 8 people living within a 20 mile radius. It is getting positively crowded around here and I can feel the changes coming. First they will want the roads kept plowed and trash hauled away and phone service and electricity by just flipping a switch instead of starting a generator or whatever. I still haven't figured out why people move out into the wilderness to get away from it all and then start immediately trying to drag it all out with them.

After I got settled down and cleaned up the breakfast mess, a huge SUV pulled into my yard, totally ignoring my subtle signs at the turnoff by the main road. The "Private Target Range, Hellooooo Targets" sign, the huge "Stop" sign. Of course, it is my new neighbors. The driver jumped out immediately as the vehicle stopped moving, a large man that would fit right into the Monday night football lineup with little problem, just starting to get a little lardy around the middle and jowls.

He gets my dander up as soon as he opens his mouth and bellows, "Howdy Little Lady." He finishes putting his foot in his mouth when he continues the bellow with, "Is your Old Man around?"

First, I am not little and few have ever accused me of being a lady. Second, I bought this bare land, built my road system and my buildings, mostly by myself, no Old Man. Not even a Young Man. Once in a while help from a friend, male or female.

This man seems to know exactly all the buttons to

push to really make points with me. He has not stopped to let me get a word in edgewise yet and just keeps lowering himself in my esteem. Now it's "I brought the Little Woman along to keep you company while your Old Man and I discuss the road maintenance around here." Uh-huh, next he will mention trash, bet on it.

The woman getting out of the SUV looked exactly like I figured anyone living around this guy would look. I know she must not have always looked like a shadow, but that was my first impression of her. Slender and fluttery, I hated the way she ducked when he swung towards her, motioning towards the house, telling her to get on in there with me while the men talked over the important stuff. Not the first time a guy was going to be disappointed that I wasn't a guy.

I've always wondered if guys think the additional weight of a pair of boobs on a woman's chest made thinking impossible for a woman. I know I have seen men stop thinking entirely when confronted with said appendages, few could ever tell what color my eyes are or even if I have eyes. They seem to carry on their part of any conversation with my chest. So, living down to his expectations, I flapped my hand vaguely toward the outbuildings while stepping back to allow the "Little Woman" into my home.

As soon as the door closed, she seemed to gain substance and character, introducing herself as Shari. I told her my name is Maxine, most call me Maxie.

Shari and Will had only been married a couple of months, having moved to Alaska from the Midwest somewhere. She was very vague about actual background and I was doing my best imitation of a non-snoopy person and didn't ask more than she volunteered. This was a very jumpy woman and I felt that she would vanish if anyone asked something she didn't want to answer.

Soon the thumping up the steps announced the arrival of Will at the door. He seemed not to be amused by the search for a guy through the outbuildings as they only consisted of an outhouse, a smokehouse and a small storage shed attached to a woodshed. Light seemed to be penetrating as he actually looked around the room, noticing only my jacket hanging with his wife's by the door, only my boots by hers, under the jackets. I didn't volunteer information so he finally asked if I lived here alone. I told him I did and asked if he would like some tea or hot chocolate or I could make some coffee but wouldn't vouch for it as I don't drink it. He settled for tea and I set out a plate of homemade cookies while we positioned ourselves around the built-in table/bench set I had made.

I don't think his eyes settled anywhere as they darted over the interior of my home. I was rather proud of it although it would not win any prizes in Home Beautiful. I built it for comfort and with what I had on hand, scrounging at the dump, picking up old materials anywhere I could find them. I did buy new insulation and new insulated chimney, but very little cash outlay was visible in it. I added on as I had the money and it is getting to be a very comfortable home. The storage areas under each seat and bench help keep the clutter down a bit and all the walls have bookshelves at least halfway up them, with my artwork above.   The bear head wearing a do-rag and granny glasses seemed to startle a chuckle out of the man and Shari started to relax a bit also.   Will didn't relax to the point of suddenly becoming chums, but there was a dim possibility of at least being civil to each other, maybe…..

Will sat there a few minutes, drinking his tea and eating several cookies before he cleared his throat and hemmed and hawed a couple of times.   Finally, shifting around on the seat, he resembled a guppy, but found his voice and offered a bit of an apology.

"Ummm, sorta stuck my foot into it when we first got here, didn't I?"

"Just a few toes, I answered.

"Maybe we could start over a bit?   Pretend I didn't just assume a whole lot?"

"Ah well, you know what they say about assuming…" and he surprised me by bursting out laughing.

"So, did you actually do all of this?"   He was slightly incredulous, but willing to listen.

"I did have a helping hand once in a while, but for the most part, yes, I did do the work here.   I have a firm belief in only building what I can afford and waiting and saving for the next improvement."   I told him.

Will and Shari were both looking at me like I had something stuck between my teeth.

Shari was the first to react, "But how do you live, here in the wilderness, with no man around to help and protect you?"

"Protect me from what?"

She was at a loss, flapping her hands to encompass everything, but no words to express it. I honestly didn't know what to make of her. Will hugged her to his side and murmured softly, soothingly to her and my first impression of him made an abrupt about face. The man obviously cared deeply for her and wanted to shelter her from anything that upset her. He could tell I was at a loss as to what was bothering her, so he murmured something else softly to her, she first shook her head no, then stopped and nodded yes.

"I'm sorry, we should explain a bit about ourselves. I first met Shari when she was married to someone else, down South. Her first husband was a good old boy to the other good old boys. But the first time I was invited to their home, she had a black eye, puffed lip, a sprained ankle and could barely walk. Fell down the steps, they said. The next time I stopped by, her other eye was swollen and turning purple, she had a cast on her arm and was favoring her other side when she walked. Fell down again, they said. I may be a bit slow, but not entirely stupid. She was scared to death of him and with good reason. She was from good family and had never been exposed to the likes of Rod. He was good looking and could pour on the charm when it suited him. Once he had her inheritance in hand and her under his thumb, he ruled with an iron rod. I really believe he would have continued until she was dead, if I hadn't sorta stole her one night when he was passed out drunk after beating her to within an inch of her life. I drove all night and got her to another state and into a hospital. The police were all set to arrest me, thinking I had done it to her, but she woke up long enough to say it was her husband and that I wasn't him. She was in and out of consciousness for several days before they were sure she would make it."

Oh Geez, now I had to rethink my opinion of him entirely. He might have some antiquated ideas on woman's place in the home, but if she was good with that, that was her problem. They looked like it suited them fine.

My morning bear must have gotten curious about the smell of charred biscuit still lingering around outside and made an appearance near the woodshed, slowly peeking around the edge. By this time the Jays had carried off all possible crumbs, so I didn't have to worry about the bear finding anything to eat, but was thinking it was getting a little too accustomed to people. I think I about gave Will and Shari heart attacks though, when I stepped out the door and shot the bear.

Evidently Will hadn't noticed the handgun on my hip. Shari about climbed his frame, so guess I should have said something first.

I took care of the skinning and butchering, bringing in the meat and stacking it on the table. I started mixing up some brine to cure the hams and shoulders to smoke later. My visitors watched wide eyed and very little comment. Shari finally asked what it would taste like. I told her if I did it right, it would be very similar to pork. The bears in this area are usually fattening up on berries, in the Fall, so fairly good eating as bears go. I offered them half the bear and they were trying to be polite and not green around the gills as they declined.   Bear isn't my favorite meal either, but I try not to waste anything.   After I had the meat in the brine, I started fleshing on the hide, to get it ready to tan.   Like I said, I try not to waste anything. When I had the hide fleshed fairly well, I salted it and rolled it up to finish tomorrow.   My guests had stayed for the whole thing.

Shari was a little pale and Will was hovering, again. I asked if they would like more tea and I was going to fix sandwiches, if they would care for some, with homemade bread.   Maybe the idea that I had just killed and butchered something had a bit to do with their refusal,   But that was okay, I figured I would see quite a bit of them, around here.

Chapter 2

The trees were budding out nicely, giving a green haze to the hillsides and the smell of fresh growing things made it hard to stay indoors. Spring in Interior Alaska is a lovely time of fast growth and renewal. From the first sign of green growth until the trees are fully leafed out is about 10 days to 2 weeks and then it is summer. This usually happens sometime in May. Daylight hours have increased to the point of not being able to see any stars. It isn't exactly sunshine all 24 hours, but the sun just dips behind a hill and right back out the other side. Summer is so short, everyone works until they drop, sleep a while and do it all over again. That is the secret to enjoying winter. It is the time to rest up from summer. By the actual first day of summer, June 21st, we start losing minutes the next day and are on our way back to winter. So everyone works.

I started seeds in egg cartons a couple of months ago, on my sun porch on the front of my house. So now I was busy getting everything transplanted into the garden I had tilled below the house. I soaked seeds of the plants not pre-started, and planted them. That would give them a week or so head start on growing also. With such a short growing season, every little bit helps.

Later in the afternoon, I heard another vehicle coming in my driveway. What is this, ignore the driveway signs day? If I had wanted people around, I would have lived in town, or at least a lot closer to town. This one is a nice looking older model pickup. Wow, a nicer looking older model driver, too. Umm, forget I said that.

If I must be interrupted, at least this one looks good while doing it. How shallow is that? But true.

The first words out of his mouth may cancel that. He is from the government, so help me, if he says he is here to help me, I may kick his shin. Okay, maybe he got that, just from the look in my eyes, he didn't say he was here to help me. He is doing some sort of survey and is looking at improving the communication system in the State. So I tell him I like it the way it is. If I wanted better communications, I would live near town. If it gets very bad out here, there are always smoke signals. He did not appreciate my attitude when he thinks he is doing something nice for us deprived Bush people. He isn't so jaunty walking back to the pickup, but the view is still good, going as well as from the front. Oh, how can I even be thinking like that. So inappropriate. He works for the Government for crying out loud. Oh well, my tax dollars at work, whether I want them to be or not. Wait, he is coming back.

He sort of hemmed and hawed a bit and finally asked if I have a phone number and when I start laughing, he grins sheepishly and says, "Yeah, figured you didn't.   But I would like to stop by and visit?"

I am not sure why, but okay.   "Sure, any time."

After he left, I kept thinking about how good he looked and he did seem nice.   But I have been fooled by seemingly nice guys before.   Even married one for a while.

The rest of the day was fairly normal for out here. I got my tiller started, after a few false starts and started tilling the garden patch.   The ground is still frozen down a ways, so will have to make do with the shallow pass over to get any recently sprouted weed seed.   Then the fun part.   I used the rake and make raised rows in the garden to plant in.   The very early started area was looking green under the plastic I put over it after I planted it in April.   After I had a couple of rows built, I used the hoe and went down the center, making a hoe wide valley with raised edges. Carrying water to the garden makes it a necessity, and this warms the soil for the roots and saves water for the plants I want, not extra weeds.   Then I uncovered the part that was growing under the double thickness of plastic and started transplanting the little seedlings over to the new rows.   Most of them were nice sturdy little plants now and already used to the cold soil and the outdoors.   The seedlings I had on the sun porch would go out into the greenhouse.

I finally stopped and realized how hungry and tired I was.   The sun was still bright and warm and it was 8 p.m., no wonder.   My outdoor shower had more than enough water in the tank from a rain shower to make a quick shower possible before going in and fixing something to eat.

If all the traffic in here keeps up, I will have to start taking a change of clothes into the shower house with me. The water drains out into a container to use it on the plants in the yard.

I finish planting my garden the next day and my back is complaining about it. Now I see why folks had large families in the old days. Short kids closer to the ground could do the planting.

A year ago, I ringed some trees down on the lower end of my property so they would dry standing to cut later for firewood. I go down and check them and they seem to be ready. So I started falling them. After I have a few down, I cut and haul them up to my depleted woodshed. Last winter had dragged on long enough I was getting worried about maybe not having enough in there. I'm pretty sure I can get enough cut and hauled in 2 weeks to have enough for the coming winter. I know, it isn't exactly even summer yet. I just like to be prepared.

After the first week of cutting and hauling, the woodshed is looking pretty good. While unloading my old pickup, I hear a motor so check the driveway and there is a newer looking pickup with a camper on the back, pulling in. I guess I am going to have to update my entrance signs, no one is taking them seriously.

However, as the guy gets out of the pickup, I may have started salivating just a little bit, it is the fellow from the government. This is late Friday evening, is he lost? Government guys don't work late or weekends.

"Need a hand?"

"Sure."

Yeah, I'm a brilliant conversationalist. He pitches wood out of the pickup and I stack in the woodshed. We finish unloading the pickup and he is sweating. Somehow, I don't think his job requires a lot of physical labor.

As we walk over to the house, he asks if I would mind if he camped here while he is doing the survey farther on out the highway. He wants a place he can unload his camper and not have to haul it all over the bad roads farther out. I offer to share my meal with him and show him where he can unload after we eat. He offers dessert. Wow, I am impressed. The man has stopped at the best place in town that makes their own ice cream and brought their home style wild blueberry ice cream out.

After we have our meal, I show him a fairly level area along the road I am hauling my firewood from. It will give him some shade, too, so the camper isn't an oven when he returns in the evening after work. The plus side is, I can't see it from the house or yard.

Chapter 3

The next day is just like a continuation of yesterday. There is never any real sunset or sunrise involved. The sun just goes behind a hill to the north, then swings around and is just as light and bright as ever. There is never an overhead noon time sun. It just circles the sky. If I can't sleep, I can always go out and work in the garden or cut some firewood.

I head down the hill fairly early but hadn't checked the time. I figured I could get a lot cut and ready to haul before I bother taking the pickup down so just cut across the yard and hike down the hill. By the time I have a couple of loads cut and dragged to the road, I would really like a break, so hike back across the hill to the house.

I dunk my head in the water barrel at the corner of the shed on my way by and it feels cool and refreshing so I am ready to fix something to eat and drive back down. I about jump out of my skin when someone says hello right by my door. Government guy is standing there and I didn't hear him coming. I better start paying attention or I may be a meal for some hungry bear. He has gone pale when I realize I have my gun out and pointed at him. Well, maybe I won't be a bear meal just yet. Reflexes still work.

I apologize and put the gun away. I ask him if he

would like lunch and he says it is breakfast time. Oops, maybe I should have checked the clock before heading out, but with daylight 24/7, it doesn't make any difference for work. I have some homemade bread I had made a couple of days ago, so sliced it and made some sandwiches which he didn't seem to mind for his breakfast. Since it was honey cinnamon bread slathered in "apple butter" made from rosehips, it was similar to a breakfast roll, anyway. I cleaned the sandwich makings up as I was using them, so after eating, I was ready to head down with the pickup and get the firewood. He tagged along, so we made short order of hauling the wood up and stacking it in the woodshed. I was surprised at how easily we fell into a routine and worked quietly but well together. I cut more wood and he loaded the pickup while I was cutting. Six full loads today. That is much more than I could have done by myself. I suppose I should find out what his name is.

When we got to the house with the last load, I went in and started the potatoes I had ready. Then we finished stacking the wood. At this rate a couple more days and the woodshed will be full. I may need to add on and see if I can have an extra year in reserve. That would certainly make me feel better. I like to have things in reserve just in case I get ill or hurt and can't go get more for a while.

When we get in the house, the evening meal is smelling very good. Maybe it is from all the work done today, or maybe it really is just as good as it smelled, but we definitely did justice to the food. A slow cooked bear roast that had marinated all night in beer then cooked in it with garlic and seasonings. The baked potatoes were good, with the brown gravy from the roast and a very small salad made from the first trimmings from the early planting in the garden. Homemade bread on the side.

I am ready for sleep when I get done eating, but government guy is relaxed and seems to want to talk. He picks up the dishes and has the dishpan full of hot soapy water before I can even say I will do them. He tells me since I cooked, he will clean up. Dang, this guy is too good to be true, he must already be married or an ax murderer just awaiting his moment.

I jerk awake as someone is carefully covering me with a throw and look straight into the most beautiful eyes. Melting chocolate comes to mind and I love chocolate. It should be illegal for a guy to have eyes and eyelashes like that. He laughs gently and says, "My name is Noah."

Oh man, did I actually just call him government guy?

Chapter 4

I wake up still slightly embarrassed by last night. Noah left right after he introduced himself and I went on in to bed. I looked at the clock and it is only 4:30 a.m. so I head on out to the woodshed and see what would be needed to enlarge it. I decide to make the shed roof into a peaked roof and just add another shed, slightly wider, on the other side. That will be simple and give me one wall already in place. I drag some concrete pier blocks over and set them up, 8 feet apart, opposite the ones I used on the current woodshed. I have some peeled logs behind the house, so drag them over, also. I will need 6 cut to 6 foot lengths. I cut them and notch the bottoms to fit the holders on the pier blocks. Then get a few peeled poles I had left from another project and I am ready to start assembly. I tack a couple of boards partway up a log to swing freely and use as braces when I get the pole into the block. Once the first one is in place, then I can nail poles across to hold it upright and straight. This will probably be the fastest woodshed I have ever worked on, since it does not require much actual extra work. The ground is already cleared and as level as it will ever be.

Noah shows up just about the same time Will and Shari pull in. They are all gaping at me like I am off my rocker. I have all of the logs up and tacked together. I will have to drag out a ladder soon, to fasten poles across the top and figure out exactly where I want a doorway. The walls will be open for ventilation so the wood can keep drying, but I do put uprights ever foot or so to hold the wood from just rolling out.

"What? Just fixing the woodshed."

Everyone came back to life and started talking at once. Will and Shari thought Noah had built it and Noah kept shaking his head saying "No."

I wanted breakfast so went on into the house and they wandered in behind me. They decided I didn't know how to ask for help. I didn't know what they were so excited about, this was an easy job. So I told them sure, I could use some help, I really hate ladders and it was about time to do some work on it that needed a ladder. I pulled a pan of hot muffins out of the oven and asked who all wanted tea or hot chocolate. I fixed the tea and chocolate, started bread pudding from the leftover honey cinnamon loaf and we all sat down and ate while the muffins were still hot.

While we ate, we discussed my new project. Everyone volunteered to help, so after we finished eating and I had covered the remaining muffins, we went out to get started. I found out quite a while back it is easier for most folks to understand a project if it is drawn out for them. So I used a sharp stick and drew what I wanted to do, in the dirt. Shari decided she would like to assist and she really got a kick out of the first nail she pounded in. No one had the heart to tell her it didn't go into anything. After all, it is the thought that counts. I found her an old carpenter apron she could carry nails in and she is happy. I turned off the oven while I was in looking. The pudding was almost done and it would finish in the hot oven as it cooled down.

By noon, we had the frame pretty much finished. When I mentioned food, everyone was more than ready. I washed up quickly and while they washed up, I chopped leftover roast very fine, added some chopped onion and pickle, added some ranch dressing and a dash of mustard and had lunchmeat ready to spread on sliced homemade bread. My early lettuce pickings were pretty much gone from salad last night, so just stirred the remaining salad into the lunchmeat mix. I had sweet tea made and fairly cool and the pudding set out for dessert.

Everyone ate like they were starving and the food was soon gone with everyone sitting back and wondering how they could eat so much. Physical labor does that to you, makes a good appetite. I cleaned up the crumbs and started some steaks marinating in a teriyaki sauce, scrubbed and oiled some potatoes and preps for dinner were done.

We were moving a lot slower on our way outside. A few sore muscles on the folks unused to working like this, had a few groans and moans. But as they moved around a bit, aches eased and soon everyone was looking at the lovely framework we had built and ready to put the roof on it. We used poles for rafters and old salvaged pieces of metal roofing on top. I did have new roofing screws to put it down with. We had a patchwork quilt affect from the different types and colors of roofing, so it was rather a different look for a roof. But to me, it was beautiful, it would work, it was paid for. Now my woodshed could hold more than double the amount it had before and since the doorway was 4 feet wide, I could also pull my small ATV in out of the weather if there was room. Since I planned on filling it entirely with firewood there would probably not be room, most of the time. I put a smaller opening for a door at the other end, so I could go in and out whichever end was handy.

I snipped some little chives on my way back into the house, started the oven and put the potatoes in. I was going to have to haul some water at the rate my rainwater was going down, unless it rained soon, I never expected this many people to be using it. While everyone again washed up out under the water tank, I fired up the BBQ.

While the potatoes baked and the steaks were grilling, I opened a couple of jars of canned coleslaw, drained them and added some dressing. I stuck some rolls I had made a couple of days ago into the oven the last few minutes the potatoes were baking and dinner on the table in short order. While we ate, a brownie pudding was baking in the oven. Noah said he had a little bit of ice cream left in his camper fridge, but wasn't sure how much. I asked him to bring it over and was taking the brownie pudding out when he came back in.

A square of the brownie, a small scoop of the ice cream and some of the hot pudding sauce from under the brownie on top, yum. A lovely quick dessert.

Noah got up and started on the dishes, Will looked surprised but went in and helped him. Shari was almost asleep. I doubt if she had ever worked so hard in her life.

Everyone was relaxed and yawning within minutes after dishes were done, so sleepy goodnights were said and all headed home after I thanked them very much for all the help. This would have taken me at least a week by myself.

Chapter 5

I get up and head down for the wood lot as soon as I wake up this morning. Lots of space to fill, now. After falling and limbing a couple of hours, I went home and had some breakfast. Then took the pickup back down to start hauling. Noah was gone when I went by his place so I figured he must have to work during the week. I cut, hauled and stacked, all day.

About the time I figured I better stop or drop, Noah pulled in and jumped out of his truck. He reached back in for 2 carry out containers and came over offering one to me. He said there was a small stand near the road and he figured since I had been feeding him he would return the favor. He didn't know what I would like, so had got me a club hoagie with chips and a huge pickle. I was wondering what I was going to fix for dinner.

He said they had the same attitude I had on getting public utilities out here. He didn't know how good business was for them, as they had some interesting signs out by the highway, very much like mine. I told him that was where I had gotten the idea for some of mine. One of these days I was going to stop and introduce myself, but figured they would feel a lot like I do about newcomers in the area.

They sure did make good sandwiches though. He

said they also offered some hot sandwiches but due to regulations, they could only offer microwave hot food. Well, this would give me a good excuse to go introduce myself, since I was a "newcomer" of sorts, only having lived here about 5 years now.   They probably felt about me the same as I felt about the newer newcomers.   Maybe my waiting a while to stop by, would be in my favor.   After we finish eating, I grab the containers and head for the trash, "Doing the Dishes, since you supplied."

We were both too tired for a late evening of visiting, so shortly after eating, we went our separate ways and some sleep.   He wasn't a bad neighbor.

The days passed quickly, wood cutting, gardening and repairing damage from the winter filled my days. Noah and I shared a few meals, but he had work to do and so did I.

I needed to take my bear hide and skull in to F&G to get it sealed before 30 days was up, so figured I would go in a couple of days.   I rough cleaned the skull and packed it in salt so it wouldn't stink.   The hide I had already fleshed and salted, so it was okay. The hams were in brine, curing to be smoked and the loins, we had eaten as roast and steaks although I don't think the neighbors had any idea they were helping eat the bear they watched me kill and butcher.

I found a nice stand of alder, so fell a few nice large shrubs and peeled.   These would make a nice smoke for the hams.   The shoulders were in the brine as picnic hams, and 4 cured smoked hams would last a good long time.

After checking the hams in brine, they looked fairly

well cured, so I hung them to drip dry and checked the smokehouse. It needed some cleaning out and I brought out the charcoal grill I used in there as a source of smoke. I started a good small fire in it, to get a bed of coals to put the green alder on and let it burn outside the smokehouse. I had some cheesecloth bags I sewed up a while back and put each piece of meat in it's own bag. By this time they had dried and had a glazed looking surface. So I hung them from the cross bars in the smokehouse, put the green alder pieces on the glowing coals in the grill and rolled it back inside and put the lid on it, tightly. A top vent and a bottom vent would keep it from choking out and it let out enough smoke to haze the air in the smokehouse. A few pieces of peeled green birch would add some good flavor, later.

I added some wood just before I went to bed that night. The smokehouse was smelling good. I sure hoped that had been the only bear in the area right now. I planned on leaving early the next morning and really didn't want to have the smokehouse raided.

I loaded the trash into the pickup and tarped and netted the whole load. No need to scatter it along the way in. The roadside looked bad enough without adding to it.

When I woke up, I grabbed something to eat on the way and a bottle of water. Then stoked the smokehouse fire again and shut it down to smolder. The meat was looking pretty good now and soon would have enough smoke for good flavor and to inhibit the growth of assorted undesirables.

I pocketed the little vial of gold I had panned out

during breakup to sell in town. I wanted to stock up on a few items. I grabbed a couple of pet carriers, just in case.

I slowed as I passed the driveway where the snack shack was located. The signs were easy to spot, even the ones for the business. The Hit & Run Snack Shack. Hmmm, wonder what that represents? Too early to stop in now, as they open from noonish until 7-ish. Yes, we should get along fine. Looks like they pay as much attention to the time as I do. Ooooo they have ice cream. I will plan on stopping in on my way home instead of some drive through in town.

I'm waiting for the guy when he opens the door for turning in the bear at F&G office. He fills out the paperwork and pulls a tooth from the skull, then measures it. Then the tags are fastened to the skull and hide and I am good to go. Now I can finish cleaning the skull and tan the hide.

Next stop is to sell the gold and see what I will be able to buy on this trip. I get quite a surprise, the price has gone way up. So maybe I will stop by the feed store and check out the chicks and some feed for them. That is something I have been wanting to do.

I'm in luck, they still have some and they are growing well. I pick out some Barred Rock and some Orpingtons, get some feed and load the chicks into one pet carrier. They get the back seat of the pickup. The feed goes under the tarp in the back.

I stop at the fuel supply and fill the 2 drums in the back, with gas and add some Pri-G from the boat shop. This will go the farthest back in the woodshed.

Then it is on to the water wagon to fill up the water

barrels and my pickup is starting to look loaded.

The member warehouse is next, to get some #10 cans of dried and canned foods. I stock up on diced tomatoes to re-can at home and to make other things with, like spaghetti sauce as it is never a sure thing to grow enough fresh tomatoes to supply all I want for the year. I see that they also have powdered tomatoes on hand, so get a couple cans of those, also. Powdered eggs, flour, sugar, salt, cooking oil, shortening, yeast, baking powder, baking soda, powdered milk, tea, chocolate, and a bag of rice pretty much rounds out my shopping there.

Then on to a regular grocery store to stock up on odds and ends. Fels Naptha soap, washing soda and borax will make gallons of laundry soap.

I find a good sale on TP so get a lot of that until I am afraid I may not be able to put much more on my pickup load. The inside is almost as stuffed as the bed and I am glad I have the tarp and net to hold everything on with a bungee cord here and there to reinforce it.

As I come out of the store, a guy is standing at the door with a beautiful big dog. He has a sign he is writing out, free dog. The dog looks at me and grins, yes, he grins. I kneel down and he puts out his paw to shake. I am sunk. The guy says his name is Pal, he is well behaved and likes to pull. He will include 3 bags of feed for the dog and a harness.

Looks like I have a new best friend. The man has to leave State and can't find anyone with the room to have him. As we load the feed, dishes and harness onto my load, 2 kids in his truck are crying and waving to the dog.   The man looks like he is about to join them.   Pal presses his face to the window looking out at them and seems like he might cry too.   I better get going, or we will all be crying soon.   Well, it isn't noon yet and I have increased my local population by about 21 new residents.

I check my mail on the way home.   It is in a row of locked boxes in the parking lot of the Fox General Store, located in beautiful downtown Fox.   Well, that is what they always say it is, I personally have never noticed the beautiful part.   It is all old tailings from back when the huge dredges went through here, mining and dumping the round gravel out the back.

Chapter 6

The trip home was pleasant and no problems from any of my passengers.   I see the signs for The Hit & Run Snack Shack far enough ahead to slow and pull in. I have been curious about this place since I moved out here.   Now I have a good excuse to pull in and snoop, er, see.

A cute little homemade cabin on a trailer frame is the first thing I notice.   It has an Open sign on it. So I pull up and stop.   I am not sure how Pal will be, so leave him in the pickup with the window rolled down a bit.

The woman at the window smiles pleasantly at me and I relax a bit.   She don't look like she is mean and unpleasant which is all I had ever heard about the people here.   Maybe they hire someone to run this.

The signs explained Hit & Run.   A mean smiling mosquito was beside Hit and an evil smiling bear was beside Run on the T shirts and hoodies.

The woman says Hi, then waits patiently for me to make up my mind.   I decide on ice cream while I am thinking, so order a peppermint bar.

I finally decide on a turkey wrap, with all the fixings. She assembles it in short order and we talk a bit about the road and the weather and assorted odds and ends. I compliment her on the food and the signs. Then tell her I had copied some I particularly liked for my driveway. She laughed and said now she knew where I lived, too. I asked how long they had lived here, and she told me 14 years. I said she must have thought it was getting too crowded when I moved in, since I was feeling that way about the newest additions.

We both started laughing and then she added about them wanting the roads kept in better shape and I about choked when we both said and we bet next was trash pickup, then electricity and mail delivery.

Pal was looking mournfully out the window and she asked if it was okay to give him some scraps she had on hand. I said sure and went to let him out. I wasn't sure if he would make a break for freedom and head back for town or not, so grabbed his leash as he jumped down. I told her I was his new person, and we were not acquainted yet. So she handed me the meat scraps she had, to give to him and begin our getting to know each other so he would expect food from only me.

Then she noticed the chicks in the backseat and we talked about chickens and how to keep them alive year around, here, without electricity. I decided I better add the chicken coop against my house, so maybe enough heat would leach into it to keep them from freezing up. If I kept it clean and made vents near the ceiling and floor maybe, it would work out okay. Insulate it very well, use Plexiglas for the windows to let in light and not much heat loss. I could put a run to use in warmer months out from that.

I figured I better head for home or my chicks would die from lack of food and water. She said she was busy mornings cutting firewood, so only had the afternoons in the shack, but maybe after she got enough firewood in, she could stop by and give a hand. Yay, I had found a friend.

Just as I was leaving, her daughter came up and said she was sorry to be late, she was finishing up today's load of firewood for her house.

The shack belonged to the daughter, the mother had just been filling in. She was building a little tiny cabin out back of the shack to rent to hikers, bikers or anyone else coming through that needed a small place overnight. I walked back with her to see it and it was so cute. A small octagon shaped cabin with a psychedelic door with a cartoon lynx face on it. She said the shape of the cabin was her daughter's idea, also the door. They had found the door at the dump and sanded it down, primed it and the daughter had done all the painting except for the lynx. It is certainly one of a kind. I like it.

Chapter 7

I start unloading the pickup as soon as I get home.
I have some old barrels with one end cut out, so put
them in a corner of the woodshed and put the bags of
dog food in a couple of them and the chicken feed into
a couple more. I use plywood covers with a handle to
keep voles and squirrels out. This enlarged woodshed
is great. I don't have to worry about everything
getting wet now. Maybe I should have made it even
bigger. I fasten a come-along to the top pole and back
the pickup over as close as possible. I hook a chain
around the top of a fuel barrel and to the come-along
and rachet it up a couple of clicks, then pull out from
under it. I have a small cart on wheels that I put under
the barrel and use a stepladder to let the barrel down
onto the cart. Then I pull it into the back corner of
the woodshed and write today's date on it with magic
marker. Then back for the other one. The water
barrels are handled the same way at the back door of
the house.

The chicks are in a huge cardboard box on the sun
porch and Pal is still on his leash fastened to a
doorframe in the house. I am not sure how he will act
around Aristotle and Socrates, my half grown cats.
Not that they are so well behaved, but one disaster at a
time. I would rather referee their meeting.

When I go in the house, I needn't have worried, the dog is laying on the floor with both cats asleep between his front paws. He is looking like the big protector. I unclip his leash and he stays where he is.

The smokehouse fire went out while I was in town, so I restart the fire and set it back in to smolder along. The meat, being fairly lean, will not require a long smoke to give it the flavor and preserve it. If this had been an Autumn bear, then it would have been extremely fat and may not have cured and smoked as easily. I would have trimmed and rendered as much of the fat as possible, but this one didn't have much fat on it. I had a small amount of the fat on ice, waiting to render when I got a chance though, as bear lard is the best for baking and deep frying doughnuts.

I look around the outside of my house, trying to decide where to add a small chicken coop to let them benefit from the house warmth a bit, during the winter. One end of the sun porch doesn't have very good growing space as I had ran out of windows when building it. Now I can just add on there. It doesn't take long to lay out a small addition. I have a lot of salvaged lumber and this will make good use of it. I think the nails will be the only things new in it. I can add the nice little touches later, but the chicks need a home, now. I think I will make a small doorway onto the sun porch, also, so I can take care of them in winter without having to go outdoors. I have a door I picked up that was probably for a bathroom or closet. Only 21 inches wide, so that will fit between wall studs. They are 24 on center.

Once the walls are up, I cover the outside of the

studs with feed bags as house wrap. That should help cut the wind a bit. Then that is covered with some old T1-11 siding and the outside is almost finished. At present, a tarp over the top is the roof. This has been one long day. There is a lot to be said for 24 hour daylight.

The next morning, I get right to work on the chicken coop. More feed bags go over the rafters I stick on and some of the better sheets of metal roofing I have stockpiled out back. I don't want this to leak. Then the Plexiglas sheets are installed as windows. I will probably wish I had made them opening, later. Maybe just add some vents I can cover in winter, on each end. I end up putting two sheets of Plexiglas with an inch of airspace between them, caulked and sealed in. That should help keep cold out in winter and also to keep heat out, in summer.

The exterior door is narrower than I thought, so I have to add another stud in the opening. Then the door is cut into the sun porch. That one I have handy, so make the space to fit and hang the door. Insulation in the ceiling and walls and a good vapor barrier over that and I start looking for scrap plywood to cover the inside so the chicks don't peck holes in the vapor barrier and get into the insulation. It won't be a pretty job, but it will work fine. While looking around for scrap, I find some old broom handles I had on hand and thought they would do well to make perches with. So they got added to the pile going up to the house. Pal wasn't sure what to make of this activity, but he came along and stayed close at hand no matter what I was doing. I'll have to see how he does on pulling loads. I have an older garden cart around here with a broken handle. Maybe he can pull it. That will have to be a future project though.

While eating my lunch, I pull tiny weeds in the garden. The chicks, already over a week old at least, should love them. They aren't sure what to do with them when I first drop them in the box with them on my way in to finish up their new home. One brave chick pecks and jumps back with a bit in its beak. Hmmm, maybe this stuff is not so bad after all and pretty soon chicks are chowing down on weeds.

By late afternoon, I have the coop pretty well finished for its new inhabitants. I put a small propane wall heater up where it wouldn't be too easy for them to burn themselves on it and run a line out the back to hook into a small propane tank, in cold weather. For now, I think the little room with its Plexiglas windows and well insulated walls and ceiling should hold enough heat to keep them comfortable. I will leave them in their big box overnight with a towel over the top, to hold their body heat in until they seem big enough to make it and before they get too crowded in the box. Part of the garden is better looking and the chicks seem happy with the new addition to their diet.

I cut some vent holes from the coop into the sun porch to screen and use for heat in the winter. I hope enough will filter through to keep my newest residents comfortable. I have some old rolls of small mesh chicken wire and build the vent frames with the wire inside to keep cats on one side, chickens on the other.

I think the chicks will be okay in the new home when they are ready. I wish I could pour a concrete layer on the floor, for easier cleaning. Instead, I have some linoleum and glue that down and partly up the sides of the walls. Maybe that will be okay for being able to clean the floors better.

This has been a productive day and I feel the chickens will be a good addition to my dream of living out here on very little income.

Before I shut down for the evening, I hike out into the woods a short distance where I had spotted an ice buildup during spring thaw. I had tied pink ribbons of surveyors tape all around the area, so I could find it again and I could see a small flowing stream of water coming out of the bank where the ice had been earlier. Maybe, just maybe, I could dig it out and have a source of good water on the property.

Chapter 8

The next morning, I take a grub hoe and shovel out to the little spring and start digging a bit about it to see if I can increase the flow a bit. I dig and pull out all the water weeds and willows I can manage. The alders I cut and dig around the roots until I have a fairly good mound of stubs and roots piled over to one side. The ground is all saturated and very mucky. I shovel out as much as I can, making a small shallow pool area. It appears to be filling fairly fast with muddy water. I will leave it a couple of days and see how it looks.

After some breakfast, it is back to cutting and hauling firewood. I had not been paying attention to the days of the week and not seeing Noah for a few days, he surprised me by showing up and pitching right in on helping with the firewood.

While we are loading the pickup, he mentions the odd sounds he had heard earlier this morning. I tell him about the possible spring I have found. The possibility of water on the place is exciting to me and I probably babbled on too long about it. I know most of the wells that have been drilled out here have been disappointing in depth and quality of water. If I can find something I can do myself, no matter what quality the water, I can purify it for drinking and cooking. That would save me a big worry and also make my gardening easier. The spring is actually uphill of my garden plot. If it wasn't, I would be laying out a new future garden plot if this really is going to be a good source of water.

After we unload the pickup, we walk over to the area I dug out earlier and I am surprised at the volume of water coming out. I decide to try to improve it in the morning, but continue to work on my wood supply the rest of today.

After we unload the wood, I fix some lunch and we take the sandwiches with us back over to the wood lot. We finish up the day cutting, hauling and stacking and I am amazed at how well we work together. Noah treats me like a partner, someone to talk to and with.   He says he is getting muscles on his muscles. We have managed to put more wood in the woodshed in one partial day of work, than I could have by myself in 3 or 4 days of steady work.

I tell him I need to go down to the river and haul some river rock to enclose the area I dug out around the little spring. He offers to haul rock from the gravel pile down the road, but I explain river rock won't leave a muddy flavor in the water. We head to the closest river and find a good, easily loaded supply of rocks. The pickup is well overloaded by the time I think we have enough.

After carefully driving the pickup between the trees, getting as close as possible to the spring, we pitch out the rocks into a pile. Somehow, it doesn't look like as many on the ground as it did in the pickup. We decide to go to the small river in the other direction, as we had loaded all the easily loaded where we were.   Noah suggested stopping at the Hit & Run for something to eat and I realized it was getting late. We pulled in and I think she was about to close up but was nice about not being obvious. We ordered a couple of cheese steaks with potato salad, chips, pickle and iced coffees. She started up the generator and fixed the sandwiches and had our order ready in a very short time. The coffees were delicious while we waited. I mentioned to her that we were hauling river rock for my new little spring and she said she had a couple of spots on her place that seemed to seep pretty good, too. She always planned on digging them out to see if it would flow freely. Now she was going to have to actually do it. She said she had some sections of new perforated sewer line, if I wanted to have a piece to bury in the rocks for the water to leach into. I offered to help dig out her seeps, we both accepted. We set a time the next morning and we went on down for our load of rocks.

I checked my spring the next morning and it was looking good. The water seemed to be flowing a small steady stream. Not a large amount, but if it remained steady, it would do fine.

Rose was waiting for me when I arrived, and we set out to the seeps she had marked. The first one was actually a fairly good seep and we marked it well with tape. Then we pulled some brush and weeds away from it. As we worked, the water flow increased a bit and we got excited to think maybe we could make springs on both places. She had paid to have a well drilled. It was over 300 feet deep and not extremely good water. They used it in the summer to wash clothes and bathe, do dishes and water the garden, but not for cooking or drinking. She had never been able to afford getting the quality tested, so wasn't sure on content.

Her spring was on a steeper incline than mine, so she could put a pipe in and have it high enough to fill containers under it. I could maybe, after I dug out a bit more around my area. She was apologetic that her backhoe was not running or she could have done this all much easier.

We took the pickup down to her storage area and found the perforated pipe. We loaded 2 pieces and dropped one by the area we had dug out for her and she got out there while I headed back to my place. She had made good use of her old dozer while it had still ran. The roads were not bad on her place, just needed some smoothing in areas. Too bad her equipment was all old and not working for her.

When I got home, I unloaded the pipe and Noah walked up. The man seemed to be a glutton for punishment, the way he just got right in and helped, no matter what the project I was working on. We carried the pipe and a chainsaw over with us to the spring site and I was pleased by the amount of water that was running.

Since I had made it pretty close to the spring with the pickup, the day before, I decided to try using it to pull out some of the stumps of the trees that were right around the spring. Each tree and shrub would drain water from the spring and the farther back I could clear, the better the chances for my water supply.

We fell a few of the small trees and then hooked

cable around the stumps and to the back bumper of my old pickup. Easing into it did nothing, so I backed up a bit and gave it a jerk. The small stump came sailing. We decided that was good and went right on to the next one. When we got to a bigger stump, we changed the cable over to hook into the trailer hitch as it was fastened to the frame and might not come loose as the bumper was. We cleared the immediate area of stump wads with the pickup and I felt pretty good about it. I'm glad none of the trees out here have a tap root or I would have just wrecked my pickup.

We went back over to the house and congratulated ourselves on a job well done. Will and Shari drove in soon after. They had brought a picnic lunch and wanted to know if we would join them. Food has always been one of my habits I enjoy a lot. Shari was an excellent cook and the fried chicken was still hot and crispy. We were just in the middle of enjoying lunch when another rig pulled in to my getting popular driveway. No one believes the signs any more. I need to get some new ones.

Noah started smiling and went to meet the new arrival. Seems it is his Dad. The 2 men walked back over and Noah introduced his Dad, Roman, all around. Soon he had a plate of food in front of him and we were all talking at once again. This is a nice older man, I wonder how Rose would like to meet him? If he is anything like his son, maybe they would hit it off. She could use some friendly male companionship, I think. Now, how will I make sure they meet?

I needn't have worried. Talk soon came around to the springs we were trying to clear out and we decided to go help the neighbor get as far along as we were on mine.   This could be perfect.

When we pull into the drive at The Hit & Run, I am sorry we just had lunch but thought we could all handle something to drink and ice cream to see us through the work ahead.

Kara and Rose are both there and we order ice creams, a couple of sodas and a couple of iced coffees. We explain what our plan is, and Rose seems dumbfounded.   I don't think she is used to having help and especially help that just drops in.   She comes along with us and I see she had moved her backhoe over to the area near the spring.   We hooked the cable around clumps of brush and she pulled with the bucket on the back.   It sure saved wear and tear on the pickups. Then the backhoe started belching out oil and she shut it off.   She said it did that as soon as it warmed up while working.   Roman hopped right up and started looking it over.   Seems he is a retired diesel mechanic. How perfect.   The 2 of them seem to hit it off right away and I must have a goofy smile on my face because Shari sidles over and grins at me then winks.   She is enjoying this, also.   She has come out of her shell. Maybe pounding nails was good for her.   Will says she is brimming over with ideas on things they can build at their place and she wants to be in the middle of building them.   Gone is the ghost and it makes her beautiful.

We leave Noah's Dad and Rose tinkering with the backhoe and head back to the Hit & Run.   Kara asks how it was going over there and we talk for a while about the projects we are doing.   She says she and her

Mom are doing pretty good on the wood for the coming winter. Will is surprised that firewood is so important to us this early in the Spring. So we both start in on him about getting ready for winter and the need for lots of firewood each year. He says he has some firewood in the woodshed that was there when he bought the place a few weeks ago. He has never spent a winter here. So since we are all out and about, we offer to go look his supply over and see what needs to be done for them to have enough for the coming season.

Noah trots down to see if his Dad is ready to go and comes back saying we can pick him up on our way back. Seems Roman is now looking at the old dozer and thinks it will be easy to get running again. Kara gets all excited and says she sure hopes so as that was a Mother's Day present from her Dad to her Mom one year. Wow, now that would be hard to beat in the present department. She said yes, Dad was really good at giving the unexpected. One year he gave Mom a rifle for Christmas, even.

We all get in our vehicles and head over to Will and Shari's. They have bought one of the places a couple of miles on down the road. The folks that had owned it wanted to move to a warmer climate. It was a nice place and Will and Shari were fixing it up to look even better. The woodshed out back was not very large and was about half full. I told them a cord of firewood is a 4' x 4' x 8' stack. We measured the pile in the shed and they may have had about 4 cord in it. I suggested they get a firewood permit from the State and not cut any of the wood on their own place unless needed in an emergency. Will saw the reasoning in that and asked where to go in town to get the permit. I told him and he made a note. Shari was laying out the area she wanted a greenhouse built. So we looked it over and I complimented her on the site she had chosen. A good south slope with no shade over it. If they hurried, they could still plant in it this season. I had some extra plants she could have for it. She said they would get the supplies needed for the greenhouse and the permit when they went to town tomorrow. I offered to come help them build if they wanted, but she said they were using a kit and it should be simple. We walked out into the trees a bit, looking for water brush and seeps to see if they may have a spring showing, also. We found some water brush, but no active seeps. We pulled a bit of brush and the roots were very wet, so we kept at it. Will brought over a shovel and dug out a bit in the middle low spot we had found. The area was very muddy and as he dug, it was getting muddier. He decided to check it tomorrow or later this evening.

We went on down to the river and loaded up the pickups with river rocks and took them back for Rose. We backed the pickups close to the area we had dug out and piled the rocks for her to use around the spring.

Noah's Dad still wasn't ready to leave as they were talking away a mile a minute. He asked Rose if he could come back by sometime and she told him, any time. He said he had some tools that could help on telling exactly what was wrong on the dozer and maybe something to help the backhoe, too. I think they like each other.

When we get back to my place, Noah and Roman go down to his camper. It has been a long busy day. I'm glad we could help Rose and Kara and maybe Will and Shari.

Noah came over a few minutes later and tapped on my door. I asked him in and he smiled and asked, "Are you setting my Dad up with the neighbor?" I smiled back and said, "I sure am."

He laughed and said, "Good, I haven't seen Dad that interested and happy since a while before Mom died a few years ago. It is like having my Dad back. Thank you. "

He reached over and kissed me a small kiss on the lips. Sparks, Wow. Then he placed his hands on my shoulders and kissed me for sure. Oh my, this guy can kiss.

He steps back and looks about as surprised as I feel. He starts to stammer an apology, then says, "No, I am not sorry." and kisses me again, gently and thoroughly. A person could get used to this.

Chapter 9

I didn't sleep too well after that surprise, last night. I knew I was enjoying having Noah around and that we worked well together, but no idea he was thinking along those lines, also.

I check on my spring and it is looking better every day. I start downstream from the source and dig out an area to gravel later for the place to fill water jugs. Then I dig carefully upstream, hoping not to ruin my little spring and see how I should place the perforated pipe.

I place some fairly flat river rocks down and then the pipe on top, gently sloping downhill. More rocks all around the pipe and out a ways on each side, trying to maintain a level surface. Then heavy duty plastic carefully on top of the rocks and foam board on top the plastic, another layer of foam board over all of that with the seams offset. A final layer of heavy plastic and I am ready to cover the whole works with dirt.

Water is flowing out the end of the pipe, so it is still going downhill. I fill the wheelbarrow with the dirt removed below the pipe and spread it over the plastic covered foam board. Then I start a ditch from the overflow toward my garden area. If I can get the water to flow as close as possible, it will save me a lot of work later.

Pal decides digging should be shared, so he gets in

and digs with me. Too bad he doesn't know which direction I am trying to go with this. I find that if I start a shallow furrow the direction I want to go, he is willing to dig in the easier dirt under the roots and moss. Maybe we can be a working team, here.

When I decide I have done enough on the water for the day and head for the house, I find that I missed breakfast and in danger of missing lunch. Guess that little project took a lot longer than I planned on spending there, today.

Pal and I eat a quick meal and I leave him in the house when I go down to cut trees. I don't want him to get hurt if I lose track of him.

I think I have almost enough wood for myself for this season and probably next, also. So I go ahead and ring some more trees to have dry wood when I need to cut next year. I am slowly clearing a good wide firebreak line around my property.

After putting away all the tools I used today, I fix a small meal and go weed in the garden a bit. It isn't very high with weeds, but I would rather keep them down so maybe I can find the vegetables as they grow. The chicks love the little weeds now and expect them when I come on the porch. The seeds planted under the plastic are growing quite well and I pick some more of the lettuce for a late sandwich, when I go back in.

After some weeding and watering in the garden and greenhouse, I head over to Will and Shari's to check on their spring.

We hike up to the spot we dug in and it has a nice little pool of water and a bit of overflow going off into the moss. They decide to go ahead and improve it so there is another source of water on their place. We spend a couple of hours pulling small brush and weeds and digging around a bit more.

As we are walking back from the spring, there is a shot off to our left a ways, but quite close. They have their property posted, so we go to investigate. It did not sound like a large caliber weapon, and with only one shot, it is hard to pinpoint the area it came from. We search around a bit and spot something red over near the trees at the edge of their property. As we get closer, it appears to be a person on the ground. We all stop and look at the body, not believing what we are seeing.

Slowly, we approach, but the person does not move. By the size and shape, it appears to be male. None of us wants to touch, but if he is alive, we should render assistance. Will finally touches the man's neck and does not feel a pulse. Shari is getting very agitated and says she thinks he is someone they know. We move to the other side for a better view of his face and Shari gives a little moan and passes out.

Since there is nothing to do for the man, we work on bringing Shari around. She is white as a sheet and back in ghost mode. "It is my ex-husband, Rod." she whispers. "He found us."

As we circle around trying not to trample the area, Shari finds a rifle. She starts to pick it up and Will and I both grab her to stop her. She is in shock and keeps saying it is her rifle that her Daddy had given her a long time ago.

If she had picked it up and it is her rifle, it would have had her fingerprints on it and her ex-husband dead on her property. I can just see the District Attorney gleefully rubbing his hands together over this one.

I offer to stay and stand guard while they go call it in to the Troopers. This is going to be messy. I feel like someone is watching our every move. I really wish I had Pal with me and a very large gun. I do have my small handgun tucked into my pants pocket and it does not show.

A pipeline security guard is driving by as Will and Shari start to pull out and he waves the guard over. Will explains the problem and the guard pulls in and drives up towards the body, but parking back a ways. He looks at the body from a distance and the rifle, but does not walk over and does not touch. He says he will call it in for us, if we like, as he is going to be in range with his cell phone pretty soon on the pipeline frequency.

I feel better with the other 2 staying here with me and the feeling of being watched fades away.

While we wait, Will and Shari talk about her ex, wondering how he found them and why he came out here. No matter how we talk it around, none of us have any answers.

Chapter 10

Almost an hour later, a State Trooper car pulls into the driveway. We stand so the officer can see where we are located. He walks slowly up the hill towards us, looking all around the area as he comes. I have met him before and he seems to be a nice, fair person, not prone to jumping to conclusions.

He has a camera and takes an occasional picture as he comes up the hill. I am sure we are all well represented in the photos for future reference. He introduces himself and asks us each our name, age and place of residence. He also has a recorder going, so nothing will be missed. He asks each of us how we came to find the body and if we know the deceased. I swear his ears perked up when Shari said it was her ex-husband.

An ambulance and another State Trooper car pulled in and he motioned them on up. Trooper Douglas relaxed a bit and the 2 Troopers walked around the body and took more pictures. Will pointed out where the rifle was and more pictures were taken in relation to where the body was. Measurements were taken and finally the body was turned over.

A quick guestimate on time of death from air and body temperature set the time of death as less than 2 hours ago, give or take a half hour. So the shot we heard was probably the one he died from. Will told them the time we heard the shot and they checked his watch with theirs for time.

As the body was being loaded, something fell out of the body's hand that had been fisted around it. Shari gasped again and fainted. Will knelt down beside her and gently smoothed her hair back from her face. The ambulance people came at once and had Will move back as they hooked her up to take her vitals. She slowly blinked and opened her eyes wide. Staring around at all of us, then the police and the ambulance and out she went again.

She slowly came around again and the look on her face was so tragic I wanted to cry. The EMT unhooked her and asked her a couple of questions and she nodded. He said something else to her in a low voice and helped her sit up. Will bent back down beside her and the EMT quietly spoke to both of them, then went back to the ambulance.

I think I guessed what Shari was going to say before I got back over to where she still sat on the ground. Her arms were protectively wrapped around her middle, like she could shield herself for the future. The looks on their faces was a study in scared and joy. The EMT had confirmed what she had thought for a while, she was pregnant. The murder of her ex in her yard, was terrifying. Just the thought that he may have been here while she was alone in the house brought shivers down my spine. Maybe this is why Will hovered all the time.

The Trooper came back over and knelt down beside Will and Shari. When he opened his hand, he held a small delicate cross on a chain in his hand. This was what had fallen out of the hand of the corpse. It had a lot of meaning for Shari and she could hardly take her eyes off it.

"The last time I saw that, it was in my jewelry box in the house, just this morning." She said.

I offered to stay here with Shari while Will and the Troopers went to the house and check it out.

I heard some cursing as they got to the door. The house had been trashed. The door was broken off the frame and inside the house looked like someone had intended to ruin everything in it. The Troopers went back to the cars for evidence kits and Will again came back and sat down by Shari. She turned her face into his shoulder and sobs shook her small frame.

We were only away from the house a little over 2 hours. So much destruction in such a short time. Of course we have no idea how many people were involved, but anger and hatred screamed out from the havoc they had created in such a short time.

When the Troopers come back out of the house, they ask if there is any place that Will and Shari can stay for the night, so they can get some help out from town. One of the Troopers will stay while the other goes in for the people and materials they will need to process the crime scene better. They do not want to leave it unattended. I am not sure whether they think we will move or touch anything or if they think someone else is still hanging around and may return and remove or change some evidence.

I offer to let them stay in my little guest cabin. It is more of a storage shed, but does have a bed in it. I lived in it until I had enough of my cabin built to move into it.

We are allowed to leave and on the way to my place, we pull in at The Hit & Run to let them know what has happened and to watch out for strangers hanging around and keep their doors locked. They offer some clothes for Will and Shari until they can get in and salvage some of their own. I don't have anything that would fit either of them.

We pulled down to Noah's camper to let him and his Dad know and left him a note, as he wasn't home.

After we got settled at my place, I fixed a quick meal that none of us much wanted. We picked at it and tried to get some down.

A short time later we all wandered off to bed, locking all the doors as we went.

Chapter 11

I had my washer and generator loaded in the back of my truck and was hauling out bags of laundry to head to the river when Will and Shari came over from the shed. I asked if they would like to go with me, but they declined. They were going to stop by their house and see if they could start cleaning it up. If not, they would go to town and pick up some clothes and groceries to last until they could go home.

I locked up my house and went on to the river and laundry day. Usually I just used rainwater at home or snow melt, but with the extra use on my rainwater and not much rain, I would just use the river.

After parking the pickup as level as possible, I dumped buckets of water in the washer and started up the generator. After it got going, I packed enough buckets of water over to do the rinse when it was time and relaxed with a good book to read. Usually winter is when I get to do a lot of reading, so it was nice getting a break.

I do 3 loads of laundry, then go home to hang them. I have clothesline stretched between trees all over behind the house. One of these days I will actually set it up better with posts and crossbars holding the lines. I have one line from the porch across a small gully to a tree on the other side with a pulley, so I can hang clothes standing in one spot.

After everything is hung and the washer put away, the generator unloaded and some leftovers for lunch, I weed in the garden and transplant from the sun porch to the greenhouse. The buckets I used at the river are full of river water, and I used it for the transplanting.

Will and Shari came back late in the afternoon. They were still not able to go into their home and after talking to the police in town, they were nervous.

Her ex-husband had flown in to town almost a week ago and 2 other men were with him. They had rented an SUV and it had not been located yet. Neither had the other 2 men. From descriptions, Shari thought one was Rod's brother, Rob and the other, his best friend, Jeremy. She said Rob was Rod's shadow and anything he did was fine with Rob. She was surprised Jeremy was with them as he seemed to always be trying to settle them down when they got too extreme in their actions.

So, there was still 1, maybe 2, people on the loose that might harm Shari, although who had taken out her ex was a mystery to all of us. Noah pulled in as we were discussing this. He had not been at his camper since yesterday morning and was just on his way back from meetings in town.

He brought a newspaper and started talking at once about the murder out in the area. The looks on our faces must have clued him in that we were aware. So then Will explained what had happened since yesterday morning to Noah.

He said on his way to town yesterday fairly early, he had seen a rental SUV parked about a mile beyond Will and Shari's place. He had not thought anything of it, figuring they had vehicle problems and caught a ride to town, which is not unusual out here.

The river was still too high for any type of fishing, although tourists may not be aware of that, so they may have been off fishing, also. We cussed and discussed all the options we could think of from the possible to the improbable and did not reach any decisions except that it was terrible and we all needed to keep an eye out for strangers in the area or anything that did not look right. There was an APB out for the rental SUV so that would probably be found somewhere soon and a vehicle stolen for transportation to get farther away, possibly. Or, they may just be parked off some small side road or unused driveway and biding their time.

I invited everyone in for dinner and rummaged in my pantry for something different to eat for comfort food. I decided on stew with dumplings and opened several jars, dumped everything into a pot on the stove and got it heating while I made dumplings.

While we were eating, Shari asked how I managed to have such a variety of food on hand all the time. So I told her about my canning and buying large cans of fruit and vegetables at the member store in town and re-canning it into smaller jars so I could enjoy it without any waste. Our climate doesn't make it easy to grow everything in enough quantity to be assured of all I wanted. She said she would like to learn how, so after dinner, we started a list of what she should have, to get started. She wants to have enough supplies on hand that they don't have to go to town every week for groceries. I tell her she will really appreciate that in the winter when the weather can turn bad easily and fast.

Will and Noah seemed interested also, so we all talked about things they could do now, to make winter easier.

We spent the evening making lists. Clothing, food, wood cutting supplies and tools to make it easier to make what they planned on building. They wanted to fix up their place to have some of the same things I had on mine and that they had noticed at the place down the road. We would look over my place in the morning so they could see how I had managed and I would let them know what I wish I had done differently.

Pal started barking and he wasn't sounding friendly about it. This was the first time I ever heard him sound mean. I looked out the window, but only saw the dust of some vehicle making a fast exit from my yard. I'm not sure, but I think it is the SUV rented by Shari's ex.

Sometimes not having a phone is not so good as we have no way to contact the Troopers. I turn on the CB radio I have in the house and we listen for a trucker going by. Maybe we can let him know and he can call the Troopers when he gets to town. None of us know whether the 2 remaining guys want to carry on Rod's agenda towards Shari or not, or if they know what type of vehicle Will and Shari drive. But if they do, they now know where to find them, since it is parked right in front of my house.

We finally contact a trucker and he agrees to pass along the word to the Troopers.

We are all a little jumpy, so we sit and talk later than we had planned. Finally everyone wanders off to their places to sleep and I check on my chicks one last time. Then Pal and I do a walk around the yard and I am carrying my old shotgun. It should discourage anyone from messing around much.

The next morning, none of us look like we got a very good night's sleep. I did get my load of firewood cut and hauled before anyone else made an appearance. While I am unloading, I smell bacon cooking and my tummy lets me know I haven't had breakfast yet. I start toward the house when Shari steps out of the little shed and invites me in for breakfast. Wow, a person could get used to this. She had bacon, eggs and French toast all set out on the little table and we certainly enjoyed it all. It's really nice eating a meal I didn't cook and has no part of a bear included in the menu.

After eating way too much breakfast, I start on the weeding. Shari and Will have a million or so questions each about what I am doing and why. I offer to help them get a spot tilled and planted as it is still early enough they could get some fresh salad greens and a few other things growing yet.

So we load up my tiller and head over to their place. We find what may have been a garden area in the past and Will started up the tiller and started making rounds of the area. It was in a very good location and they should have no trouble growing things there. While we were working the area, Will, tilling, Shari and I throwing rocks, a Trooper pulled in. He came over to where we were working and we all took a break and told him about the SUV in my yard the evening before.

He did give us an update on the murder and told Will and Shari they were free to go back into their home, now. I don't think Shari was too happy to go back in, knowing 2 of the men were still at large. I offered them the shed until the house could be all cleaned up and things put in order. She jumped at the chance.

Rod wasn't shot with the rifle, like we had all thought, he had been stabbed in the back. But his prints were all over the rifle. The knife was from her kitchen. It had a partial print, but not matching hers or Will's. The Trooper sort of looked at me, but I quickly pointed out I had been with them at the time.

The Trooper left and we went back to the garden spot. Will said they had garden tools back in the shed behind the house, so he went to bring some out. After he brought rakes and hoes and shovels out, we got busy making fairly straight rows although there is more planting space in crooked rows. They didn't buy my idea so we did the string and stakes thing to make straight rows. It did look nice when we were finished.

Will offered us lunch at the Hit & Run, so we headed over there and brought them up to date on what we had learned. Seems Noah's Dad was hanging out there for the day, working on the old dozer. Rose was working on a small cabin and Kara was running the snack shack.

Roman came walking up the hill while we were still there. He said he needed a couple of tools he couldn't find in his stuff in his truck. Kara yelled over to her mom and she came over to see what was needed. She wasn't sure if she had what he needed, either, so they went down to her storage area to see what they could find.

They came back fairly soon, and told us someone had been in the old storage unit she kept things in. Looked like they stayed overnight in it. The storage unit was a section of one of the old pipeline camps, an Atco unit. It wasn't in good condition, but there was still a bed in one of the rooms and it had been used.

Roman and Rose seemed to be hitting it off fairly well. They had both lost spouses to death and were alone. They both liked to work and got pleasure from a job well done. Hmmmm, seems like maybe we should be edging them together a bit more. Now what to do for her daughter?

"Hey, Noah, do you have a brother?" Oh sheesh, why did I ask that?

"Well, as a matter of fact, I do," he answered. "Why?"

"Oh, just curious." Me and my big mouth.

Noah came over where I was sitting on a bench and sat down beside me. He picked up my hand and held it while looking at me with those darn melted chocolate eyes. "I was going to ask you if you minded if my brother came out and joined Dad and I." he said.

Okay, this was just too perfect. If he was even half as nice as his brother and Dad, they were a bunch of guys just needing pounced on.

Roman said he was heading to town to pick up his tool trailer and just bring it out. He had a lot of supplies that would make repairs on the old dozer and backhoe much easier and he needed a place to park the trailer as he now had it in storage and they were charging him a bundle to store it.

Noah walked over and spoke to his Dad a couple of minutes, they parted and Roman headed to his truck and left.

I figured I had spent more time socializing the last couple of weeks than I had in the last 5 years and had better get home and back to work. Even though we were all stuffed from lunch, Will picked up ice cream for each of us as we started back to his SUV. I'm going to have to get busy or not fit into any of my clothes.

While the tiller was still running after unloading it, I took it around between the rows in my garden. I spotted several plants that needed thinning out a bit, so after parking the tiller, went back with a flat and trowel and dug up a few here and there. These would jump start Shari's garden for her. As I dug each plant, I labeled with magic marker on a plastic fork handle and stuck it in the flat beside the plant. That should save her being too surprised at what was growing in her garden later.

When she came out of the shed and saw what I had fixed for her, she started to cry and laugh at the same time. I wasn't sure what to do. She sputtered a bit and said she guessed it was raging PG hormones or something but that was just so nice of me and she was just so happy to be living near so many nice people. Will came over and patted her back a few times and I could tell he was as clueless as I was.

They decided to go right back over and set out the

plants so they wouldn't wilt down.   They took a jug of manure tea I had mixed up and I told them to pour a small amount under each one before setting it in the hole and covering the roots, then watering them in.

After they left, I worked some more in the garden and greenhouse.   As the afternoon progressed, I started getting a feeling like I was being watched. After the events over at Will and Shari's, it made me more nervous than usual, so I worked my way toward the house and right on inside.   I think I better start keeping Pal with me all the time when I am outdoors now, even if I have to tie him to keep him safe while I am falling trees.

Chapter 12

Oh, I am in so much trouble now. Seems that melting chocolate eyes are in my dreams now. Yeah, he is nice, yeah, he is thoughtful, yeah, he is very easy on the eyes. Hmmm, where is the downside of this? Town job? Wife or girlfriend stashed somewhere? No, he said he wasn't married, so no wife as I don't think he is a liar.

Well, those were certainly not my usual morning wake-up thoughts. I better get back to work. Pal and I take the pickup down and load up most of the firewood I have cut. I loaded, he brought me sticks.

My woodshed is looking so much better. It is almost entirely filled, new larger extension and all. I do have the little area inside for pet food and tools, but it is now holding at least 2 years' worth of firewood. I grab the saw and go back down. I hate to kill so many trees, but I need to ring them for cutting next year to fill the space of wood used this coming winter. By the time I need to get started on the evening meal, I think I have enough ringed for the next season. Now I can relax a little bit and work around the place on other projects needing done.

I want to expand my ice cellar a bit or build another one which would probably be the best way to do it and not lose the ice I have from last winter. It makes great storage for fresh goods and helps out during the summer. I even have a place picked out to build another one. Mine is quite small as I was in a hurry when I built it.

When I get back to the house, I find an old tarp and drag it over to the area I want to dig out. I measure out the area I want to dig out and start by cutting around the edges with a very old chain and bar on my chainsaw, just in case I find rocks. The chain is beyond sharpening and has missing teeth, so I am not ruining a good chain and bar. Then I cut a grid through the whole area so I can remove each section of cover foliage onto the tarp and replace it over the ice house when I am finished. This is probably not a good use for the saw, but it sure speeds up the job.

I start at the edge of the bank of cut squares and carefully pry one loose from the frozen soil under it. I use the wheelbarrow and move it over onto the tarp. They won't have to go back exactly as I removed them from the grid, but may fit better, if I am careful with them.

After a while, it is going really well and I have most of the foliage removed when Will and Shari come back from cleaning and planting at their place. They immediately want to know what and how I am doing this new project. So I explain how I am digging it out, making a gravel floor, and building heavy pole wall sections with rough cut boards behind the support poles. A vapor barrier and foam board insulation behind that and another layer of vapor barrier and another of foam board if I can afford it or find more.

The roof will be done the same way, only stronger as moose may walk over it. All the dirt I will dig out will be mounded over top of the whole works, the foliage placed back over it all and left open in winter to freeze as much as possible inside. The entryway will be a double door set up, like a storm lock. An outer door, a hallway and an insulated inner door. I am going to try setting some LED lights along the ceiling of the entryway and inside the room going to a battery setup and solar panels if I can. The gravel floor will be fine for melting ice in Summer.

I will put jugs and buckets half full of water in the room as I get them, so they can all freeze in winter and slowly thaw in the summer, keeping the room as cool as possible. As usual, I will also make an area to store a sleeping bag, tent and some food items in moisture proof containers so nothing molds or mildews and to keep rodents out.

If my home ever catches fire, I don't want to be stuck out here with nothing in the winter. I don't mention that I will also stash a gun or two and ammo out here. I like planning ahead for any emergency and who knows what types of emergencies may arise? This bank I am digging into is mostly permafrost so if I am careful and speedy on my project, maybe I won't make it thaw too much and it will help keep my ice house frozen year around. By using the old chainsaw, I am making great progress on digging out the space I want. The dirt is wind blown silt and frozen, so no rocks at all in it. It does work like sandpaper on everything, so I clean and oil the saw very well every time I fill the fuel tank. If I were building a root cellar, I would plan on leaving off the foliage and planting the roof to some nice plants for food.

Will wants to try doing this over on their place and Shari likes the sound of having ice all summer. I tell her for ice to use, they have to cut blocks of clean ice in the winter and store them up on pallets or something so they don't get dirty on the gravel and insulate them with sawdust or something to keep them frozen and chip off pieces in the summer to use.

I don't do that as I just keep soft drinks and juice out in mine and my drinking water near the door in it, in the summer. In the winter, my sun porch is cool enough to be a large walk-in fridge and the other porch is a freezer. I can keep some lettuce and greens growing on the sun porch, but not much likes it that cool. But it gives me fresh green food in winter and I do sprouts, too, for a change in my diet.

Will helps carry blocks of dirt to stack on the 2nd tarp I have set out and the hole is going much faster. I decide to slant the floor a bit toward the front, so any possible water will run out instead of pooling inside. My old saw blade and chain are about shot though. This would have taken me weeks at least to dig out by hand, maybe more as I would have had to wait for the ground to thaw and only managed a few inches ever couple of days in depth.

I cut a small trench from the lowest floor area out to the side to make a drain in the floor. Someday, I may be able to pour concrete and it would be easier to place a drain now, than later. I have the pipe, put it in place and put a can over the end sticking up in the floor and another over the outside end, just so we pay attention to where it is.

I mark out where I want the actual walls to go and

start notching poles to nail in place for the framework. My stomach starts complaining and only then do I notice it is after midnight and I haven't even had lunch yet. Twenty-four hours a day of daylight does mix up meal times. No wonder I am so tired and now that I am thinking about it, starved.

I open a couple of jars of white chili and get it heating up and go take a quick shower. I am really looking grungy from today's work. The white chili is heating nicely, so I cut some thick slices of bread and butter it, then toast it on the griddle. Looks like I need to bake again, tomorrow.

Will and Shari come in just as the bread is perfectly toasted and we all sit down and eat. Shari has decided she wants to learn as soon as possible how to can. She really likes having a meal ready in just a few minutes. I can see we will be doing canning lessons soon.

When I wake up the next morning, I get right on the ice house job after mixing up a batch of bread dough
I have to hurry on this job or the bank will thaw and slough down. I haul all the junk plywood and boards I have piled out back over, and start putting them up on the outside of the pole frame we put together last night. Then I put a good vapor barrier plastic around the walls and then assorted foam board pieces. Then another layer of plastic to keep the foam board from soaking up water although it is claimed that it doesn't. When I start putting the blocks of dirt back, I try to do it evenly, front, back and each side, so no side gets more pressure against it than another. The blocks are getting soft, so the easy work is about to end.

I remembered the bread dough I had left rising in the house and ran back in. Sure enough, it had over-risen and was flat in the bowl. I punched it around a bit, added some sugar sprinkled on it and hoped it would respond. While in the house, I fixed something to eat before heading back out.

Now came the fun part. Figuring out what type and shape of roof I wanted to put on the ice house. I wanted it to blend in a bit with the surroundings, so decided to try making it shaped a bit of a dome. One last chore for the poor old bar and chain on the saw. I cut out a hole in the middle of the floor, found a nice large flat rock and dropped it in the hole and went looking for a good spruce log. I had a nice 10 foot long one, on pallets behind the woodshed. I drag it over and then found the roofing compound. I liberally coated the bottom of the log with the tarry looking gunk, then wrapped it in some old rags and coated them, also. I tacked 2 2x4's on the sides of the log, then slowly set the end over the hole and started raising the log.. As it went up, I kicked the 2x4's along, to act as braces. Once the log was upright, I check it with a level and it isn't too bad. So I tamp the dirt back around it that was loose inside on the floor, checking once in a while for straight. This is not a beautiful job, but it should work.

I checked on the bread again, and it didn't look too bad, so shaped it into pans and left to rise again after turning the oven on to preheat. I would have to pay attention this time.

I drag a few more poles over to use on the ceiling, then put the bread in the oven. I take care of the chicks and open the little door so they could go out into the small run I had built for them. They are cautious at first, then all go out. They are starting to get feathers and look lanky. By the time they were all outside, I could smell the bread, so checked it. Still needed more time, so I picked up some in my cabin so it looked neater and put the dishes away. By then, the bread was ready to come out. So put it on racks to cool and went back to work.

Using the step ladder, I put the first few poles up on the post I had placed in the middle of the room. I spiked them in place on top the post, then went around the sides and evenly spaced the ends over the walls. As an after thought, I placed a square box to allow a chimney in future if needed, through the roof and nailed it firmly in place. I put it back by the back wall so it would be inconspicuous. Then I put a small section of insulated stove pipe I had found at the dump in and screwed it in place. While I was at it, I made a couple of vent boxes that I could close up with foam board so it wouldn't get too warm in there, later.

I crisscrossed the roof with more poles, making it look like some primitive housing project. I hoped it would add strength to the roof, just in case a moose did try walking on it. Then I added some of the junk salvaged plywood and OSB. Tacking it down, here and there. I could walk all over the roof without it sinking in or swaying. I covered the whole works with vapor barrier and tacked it over the sides and ends of the poles after trimming them to length where they hung over. I used some more of the roofing compound around the chimney piece and wrapped the plastic tight against it, then rags and more roofing compound. I used a can of the fire retardant spray foam inside the wooden box against the chimney so it should be insulated okay. I would place a chunk of foam board over and fasten one to the inside of it unless I needed it at some time.

More foam board pieces and sheets on top of the plastic and yet more plastic. Then comes the dirt. My dirt chunks are coming apart fairly well now. So I brought the wheelbarrow over and use it to move most of the dirt up onto the roof. Then it is spread around gently to not puncture the roof materials. I think I will need to plant or build a fence to deter moose. The hooves may puncture, also.

By the time Will and Shari show up from their trip to town, I am ready to call it a day. I am not done, but I can see the end of it soon.

Chapter 13

I think they must have maxed out credit cards or had a lot of cash on them. The SUV is loaded and then some. Shari has her new canner and lots of #10 cans of fruit and veggies to start learning to can on. She has cases of empty jars and some empty flats from the plants they had bought in town and planted at home before coming over. They planned on planting the bag of sprouted potatoes they had bought, tomorrow. That being the first of June, they should have a good garden from it all.

They had also made an appointment for her to see a doctor to check on the baby. They had already decided to move to town the month before the baby was due and stay until it was about a month old before coming home.

We unload most of the canning stuff into the little shed they are staying in and would bring it over to my cabin as we use it. Maybe a canner load per morning, before we get started on regular chores for the day. They insisted I get half, as I was taking my time to teach them and we finally settled on I supply my own jars.

I was surprised the next morning to see Will ready to learn right along with Shari. Yes, I have revised my opinion of the man big time. He might be a cheechako, but he was willing to learn. I decided fruit would be the best and easiest thing for them to learn.

So we re-canned peaches and pineapple. I get out my canner too, so we could finish faster. I started a large pot of water heating to rinse the jars in and put the lids in a smaller pan of water on a back burner.

Soon we had all the jars sparkling and ready to fill. We opened cans and filled jars, wiping the rims and putting the hot lids on and then the bands. We are using the pressure canners as water bath canners for fruit. They work well for this and if in doubt, let the pressure build up to 1 pound before shutting them off at the end of processing time.

We have breakfast while the canners are processing, and then place the hot jars out on towels on my counters to cool, covered with another towel to keep drafts from the hot jars. The hot water from the canners is poured into the dish pans and used to wash and rinse dishes. Then let cool down and would water plants with it after it was cool. When you carry water, you conserve.

The water from the spring I had dug out was slowly inching closer to my garden area all the time, so maybe I wouldn't have to pack water for that, soon. Then my rainwater system would do most of the water needs for the house during the summer. If the spring cleared up enough, I would be filling buckets for winter and storing them. It didn't have high volume, but it was steady. Maybe I should try digging out a large enough hole to dip a bucket here closer to the house, line it with river rocks so no mud in it and have that handy. Maybe the next project.

After the canning is done for the morning, I go back to my ice house project. They are amazed at how it is coming together and we set up a bucket brigade and get the rest of the dirt on top much faster than I had been doing it. Then we start on the foliage squares. It is a good thing I cut them fairly small or we would not have managed as well as we do. They have stayed frozen better than the plain dirt chunks because of the plants and root system on them. I put an upside down bucket over the chimney in back before I started the dirt last night and no one even asked about it as we placed the plant squares around the roof. Soon it is ready for the doors and I stuffed a sheet of foam board in the hole and left it there while I rounded up the supplies to make the doors. It is still pretty cold in there and I want it to stay that way.

I have an old insulated metal door down behind the lower storage shed, so go to check on it. I thought it would do well for one of the doors, a homemade one would do for the outer door. I make a frame of 2x6's to hang the door and another one to drop down inside to keep the door closed. It would work on a hidden latchstring on the wall. I bolted the hinges through the door, so it was fairly sturdy and might keep a bear out unless he was determined. The chimney would be the weak link in this building. I planned on planting some small spruce trees around the edges in back and maybe fairly close to the chimney or at least enough to confuse the outline a bit. Maybe make a couple of metal cutouts to plant there, to look like trees unless checked up close.

That evening, when Will and Shari came back from cleaning on their house, they told me they would probably be able to move back in it in a couple of days.

But was it okay to stay until then and continue the canning lessons? I said sure. I was getting used to having them around and hadn't seen Noah in a few days as he was taking care of his survey farther out and not coming back each evening. I was getting used to neighbors.

After our evening meal, we went over for ice cream and visited with the women there for a while. Roman was due back in a couple of days with his tool trailer and would be parking it there, while he worked on the equipment. He had asked to rent one of the small guest cabins while he was there. Rose said she thought he was earning the use of a cabin with all his work. He told her it was the most fun he had had in years and what was the price for a cabin. We were waiting to see how that turns out.

After visiting a while, we went on over to Will and Shari's house to see how things were looking in the garden and the greenhouse they have started. It is assembled and ready to plant the plants they have picked up in town. We look it over and talk about how much room some of the plants will need, and set about planting as we talked. We soon have it all planted.

As we walk around the garden plot, the smell of the old outhouse out back, is a bit strong. Guess a person would have to only work out here when the wind was the right direction. There is a newer one closer to the house that is in use now. No wonder they built a new one.

We go back to the house and it is nice seeing it all neat and clean again. They have done a lot of work on it in the last several days.

We talked about their spring and they said they have not had time to do any more work on it yet. But it is on their list. Their list is getting as long as mine. They are excited about doing the work themselves as much as possible. Neither have experience but they figured if I could, so could they.

They want to build an addition onto the house and make another bedroom and a pantry. I always wondered why the folks that built it and lived in it for years never added a pantry, anyway. Living this far from any town could get difficult to get groceries or other supplies if the weather turned bad. We look at the area they want to add on to and check for how it could be added to the roof. There is a window there so that could be the space to put a door. They decide on size and we start a material list for them to pick up in town next trip in. Their house is on a compacted gravel pad so adding to the house should not be a problem.

I go to sleep that night and dream some more about melted chocolate eyes. It doesn't help that his voice goes right along with the eyes. Dang, that guy can kiss.

Well, that wasn't exactly a restful night's sleep. So I am a little grumpy the next morning when I go out to the garden and pick weeds for the chicks. But watching them zoom around their little pen chasing mosquitoes and each other and the weeds I toss in has me in a better humor by the time Will and Shari show up for today's lesson in canning. They look like they had a rough night also and Shari is still a little green around the edges.   Seems morning sickness has struck.

She is feeling fine now and we get right to work on the peas, corn and string beans she has picked up in town.   They have to process longer at 10 pounds of pressure but with the canners we have, once they have started timing, we can go outside and do other things until the time is up.   She wants to learn to do meat, also, so whenever we get something to can, we will have more lessons.   She is amazed at how easy it is.

We built the insulated outer door for the ice house while the canners worked indoors.   She uses her cell phone as an alarm and it went off before we were totally done.   We go in and turn off the stove and left the canners to reduce pressure at their own speed and back out to finish our project.   When we go in about a half hour later, the gauges are down to zero so we take off the rocker weights and open the lids.   Again we placed the jars on towels and then cover them and use the hot water for my pan of dishes.   The canners are dried out and placed to finish cooling on the cold heater.

We are just coming out of the house when a vehicle pulled into my yard.   It is a neighbor from farther up the road and they are upset.   Someone has broken into their storage shed and stolen food and some gear.

We all feel a small shock to realize we were becoming complacent about the 2 guys still possibly in the area and the unsolved murder.   We all talk it over and no great ideas popped up.   They didn't think it was enough stuff to make a trip to town for, but wanted everyone in the area to know there are thieves or a thief around.   They did ask if we would let any

Trooper that wandered by, know. We said we would and they headed back home.

We figure we better lock up every time the houses are left unattended. Even if it was just while we are working out of sight of the doors. I think I better fasten a key to my pants pocket or I will be losing mine and have to break into my own house. That would be embarrassing.

Will and Shari head on over to their house and I go back to work on my ice house project. I transplant some small chokecherry trees around the edges of the roof and set some currant bushes near the chimney so make it harder to spot. Moose don't eat either one, so thought maybe that would help keep them away from the roof. As the small trees grow, I will interlace the limbs to make it more of a fence. Figuring I wouldn't want them to go up the front area either, I plant more of the small seedlings around the whole place except the door. A few of the seedlings are actual cherry seedlings that grew from seeds and are about 3 years old. I know they won't grow true to type, but any will be better than none amd make good jelly. I plant all the seeds from fruit I buy in town. Just maybe I will get some apples, pears, plums and cherries that survive the weather here. The moose and voles are my main problem although many of the seedlings die the first winter from the cold. However, a few of each is struggling along.

I pick up my tools and put them away for now. I want to do a bit of work on the inside of the building, build some shelves along the inside walls. I plan on building them sturdy enough they could be used to sit on. I may have to pick up some lumber to make the shelves as all my projects have used up most of the spare stuff I had laying around.

I measure out the spaces I want to build and write down the materials list as I go. It is all short and small pieces, so maybe I can scrounge up enough to do the job.

Pal starts barking and I go check. There is dust hanging in the air from a vehicle that has evidently just backed around the drive out of sight. I hate things like this. Is it just an innocent snoop that don't believe the driveway signs, checking out the road or is it the rental SUV with the other guys in it from Shari's ex? Or just some jerk? I am so glad I have Pal, now. He certainly is good at letting me know when anyone is around.

I take the pickup down to check my assorted building materials. With the list and tape measure in hand, it doesn't take long to pick out what I will need to get started. I have more on hand than I thought I did. After loading the pickup with the pile of materials, Pal and I drive back up to the house. After unloading, we go into the house. The cats are acting jumpy, so I pay close attention and soon spot something moving through the brush and trees out across the yard. Watching closely, I see a man sneaking through the trees. I open the window over the table and fire a shot into my wood pile. The man dives over the bank and I hear cussing and crashing as he bolts down the hill. Anyone sneaking through the woods around here is not my friend. If he had walked right up to the door and knocked, I would not have reacted that way.

Noah pulls in a while later and I tell him to be watching for some guy out in the woods. And that I had fired a shot into the woodpile since he was sneaking through the brush. Noah looks a little funny at that, but doesn't say anything except to be careful. I'm planning on that.

While I'm working on my shelves, I hear Pal bark again. Dang, Grand Central Station around here. I go out to see what's up.

A State Trooper vehicle. Hmmmm, wonder what he wants?

It seems the person on my place earlier, called me in. I ask the Trooper if it is illegal to shoot my woodpile. He says it isn't and I show him where the shot hit, right on the target I have set against the pile. Then I explain the circumstances and also mention the thievery at the neighbors. That and the murder and all my signs around the place should make it open season on snoops. I asked if he had noticed the Private Target Rang, Helloooo Target sign at the driveway and he said he did. So why is someone that is sneaking through my woods complaining about me? Because I didn't hit him? Seems the guy thought it was a shortcut down to the river to fish. He lost a bunch of tackle and his pole when he dove over the bank. Myself, I think it was cheap at the price, I could have hit him, easily. I tell the Trooper, if the man has the guts to come apoligize and hunt for his stuff on his own, he can have it back. The Trooper is laughing as he leaves to go check out the theft at the neighbors. I go back to building shelves.

When everyone comes over, later, I tell them about the guy and him calling the police on me. I have seen more Troopers out here in the last few weeks than I have seen out along this road in all the years I have lived here.

They find it hard to believe the guy had the nerve to call me in to the police. He was obviously in the wrong. So when he shows up later, to apologize but with attitude, he is surprised to find I am not alone and my friends think he is an idiot. Shari tells him if he can't see where he is in the wrong, maybe a load of buckshot in his tail will help him understand. Wow, she is certainly finding herself out here. Then she tells him about the unsolved murder and the thievery in the area and a dim light starts glowing in the recesses of his brain. Then it dawns on him that I could have shot him and been in the right. He about passes out. Will is so proud of Shari, he is about popping buttons.

I do tell the man if he ever sneaks through my yard again, to expect to have a worse reception.

Chapter 14

Will asks if they can borrow my tiller to till between the rows in their garden, so we load it in my pickup and take it over to help out. They ask if we can enlarge the garden area a bit, by just tilling a few more strips around the outer edge of it.

About the time we are finished with the new improved garden, the wind changes and that horrible outhouse odor hits us again. I suggest they pick up some lime in town next trip because that is the worst I have ever smelled. They agree.

I spot a large bear in the edge of the woods beyond the outhouse, and tell them. They have not seen any around here, except the one I shot the day we met, so they are interested in seeing one. I do tell them a bear can be dangerous and be very careful about any food around the place. Once a bear finds food, they will keep coming back to see if there is more.

This bear just stays back in the edge of the trees, not coming closer, and sniffing the air. Then it drops out of sight.

We have one more morning of canning to do, so they decide to spend the night as they have been doing and we can get a nice early start in the morning.

We stop at the Hit & Run on our way by, and just make it as they are about to close. We offer to just get ice cream so they don't have to stay longer but they laugh and say they were closing early as they were tired of sitting with no one to talk to.

We talk over the thefts that have been occurring around, as there have been a couple more in the area that we have heard about. It seems to only be food and not a lot at each place. Almost like someone is trying not to take too much from any one person. Well, if we must have a thief, it is nice to have a thoughtful thief.

I told them about my little occurrence yesterday. Kara starts laughing and says she told the guy the only access to the river was back by the bridge and there were very few, very small fish in it anyway. He had started to drive on past her shack to use their driveway which also does not access the river, and she told him he would probably get shot by her Mom if he continued. He was muttering about inconsiderate people as he backed out and turned around. Well, he certainly was one of those, himself.

While we were eating and talking, Roman pulled in with his tool trailer. Oh my, he has a huge enclosed shop type trailer. He could rebuild anything he sets his heart on. Rose shows him where he can park it, and level it so he can use it as a shop. She is going to have a small village here, soon. Seems he has a small room with twin beds in the end of the shop trailer. He used to travel to jobs and stay in the trailer while he worked. He has another guy with him that is helping him set it all up.

The guy resembles Roman and Noah a little bit. But he is very tall and lean, not skinny, just not an ounce of fat on the man. He has muscles though, as he lifts the blocks to level the trailer with ease. When they come back over, Roman introduces his son, Thaddeus. Known as Thad. The guy is certainly a nice looking guy. Wonder if he is single? Is he is going to help his Dad? What? He drove a 4x4 pickup out, as pilot car for his Dad's trailer.

They each order a sandwich also, so it looks like a good thing we showed up to keep the shack open later tonight. It will be closer to 8 pm before they can close tonight.

While we are all sitting around talking, a Trooper pulls in. He walks over and asks for Will and Shari. Will stands up and walks over to him and they converse in low voices a few minutes. Will looks shaken. He asks the Trooper a question and they walk over to all of us.

The Trooper says he was on his way to town when he saw a bear tearing up a small shed up the hill from Will and Shari's house. He stopped to investigate and the bear dragged something out from the rubbish. From what the Trooper could see, it was a human body. So he loaded his riot gun with slugs and shot the bear. He wanted to know if anyone there would come ID the body if possible. He had called it in and a crew were on their way out to pick up and work the scene. But it looked as though the body may have been there since the day the other body showed up. It was not a pretty sight and may not be able to ID it from the way it looked.

Oh my, no wonder that outhouse smelled. I am so glad we had not decided to go use it or check on it. I guess I shouldn't feel that way, but I certainly didn't want to find something like that.

We all load up and head over to see if anyone knows or can recognize the deceased.

The Trooper is right, about all we can tell is that it probably is male. Although Shari says the size is right to be Rod's twin brother, Rob.

If so, that only leaves the friend, Jeremy, on the loose in the area, if he is still in the area.

I wonder if that is who is responsible for the food thefts in the area? He must know he is being looked for. I suggest it to the Trooper and he agrees.

Later, when the team has searched the area and through the outhouse remains, they find another rifle. Shari can identify the rifle, it belonged to Rob. So tentatively, he is ID'd as Rob.

Shari is very nervous and says with their Daddy being a county sheriff back home,that he will be out for revenge when he learns his sons are dead. He was the main problem with her getting help when she had been married to Rod.

She went in the house and brought out the paperwork and photos that were taken when Will got her to a hospital the last time and also the copies of her divorce papers. She showed the Troopers and explained what had been an on-going problem and what she was afraid would happen now, with his family. The Trooper said they would keep an eye out and they did not allow such abuse no matter who his Daddy was.

We were a somber bunch when we left there. We dropped off the ones that rode with us, at Rose's driveway and went on to mine.

It seemed that maybe Jeremy was protecting Shari

from Rod and Rob in a twisted sort of way. Who else would know they were even there, let alone on Will and Shari's place? Who else could get that close to them, and how did he get so close to both of them, after the first one was down?

We proceeded with the canning the next morning and Shari and Will were both confident they could can fruit and vegetables on their own, now. When any of us got meat to can, we would have another lesson on canning, but if they followed the directions in the canner book, they would do okay.

We all left soon after the canners were done and they went to their place and I went for a load of gravel for the floor in the ice house. It is thawing enough to be muck soon in there. I put down a layer of plastic and some old rugs I had picked up here and there. The gravel would go on top and the rugs would keep it from sinking in too much. I tacked screen over the vent openings made earlier as the roof was being put on. No reason to be bitten by bugs while working in here. I should have figured out a way for a skylight or a window somewhere, but that would defeat my purpose for an ice house.

The gravel pit isn't too far away, so my load doesn't take very long to load as I use 5 gallon buckets so I can dump it exactly where I want it. Unloading takes just as long as loading, as I tend to wear out after a while. So I go fix lunch.

I start a batch of bread dough while I am in the house. Maybe I won't forget it today and it will be nice for some cinnamon rolls. These won't be fancy, just regular rolls.

While the dough is rising, after my lunch,   I go spread gravel inside the ice house.   I think I will need another load to finish the job nicely and some around outside the doorway, also.

I go punch down the dough and head for another load.   I won't be able to dawdle on this one.   So I really shovel into the buckets.   The dough is just right, when I get home, so I park the pickup and go take care of the bread.   One loaf and some dinner rolls, then the rest into cinnamon caramel rolls.   I make the loaf and the rolls and set them to rise and the oven to preheat.   Then flatten out the rest of the dough and spread it with some corn syrup, then sprinkle well with cinnamon and a lot of brown sugar.   I cut them fairly thick and place in a well buttered deep sided baking pan with brown sugar and corn syrup sprinkled over the bottom.   After the pan is full, I slightly flatten them with my hand and set them to rise.

The bread is ready, so are the rolls, so they go in the oven.   I think the ice house will feel good, after working in the house and baking on this hot day.

With all the sugars, the cinnamon rolls are almost ready to go in the oven so I move things around in there so they will fit.   While the breads cook, I go back outside and spread some gravel around in front of the doorway.   With the windows open, I can smell the bread baking and soon the cinnamon rolls, also.   The smell must have made it quite a ways, because as I am taking them out of the oven, Noah, his Dad and brother pull in.   I put 3 hot cinnamon rolls on plates and a dab of butter on top to melt in and hand them each a plate and fork as they walk in the door.

Thad looks at his Dad and brother and asks if it is always like this? And why did it take them so long to let him know?

Noah's job is over, it was only temporary anyway. So he is at loose ends. Thad just finished his job as Inspector on a large building project going on at the University in town. Roman is retired, so the guys have the rest of the summer to do whatever they please. They really are pleased to eat good food, so we box up a couple of the cinnamon rolls and head over to talk to Rose and Kara.

While we are all eating, the guys offer to help out around both our places in exchange for a place to stay and meals once in a while.

Oh yeah, how perfect is this? None of us have had good luck on the folks we thought were going to help us out here. Now 3 gorgeous guys just drop in on us and offer help. I think we can handle that. I know I can. Kara and Rose look stunned as they eat their rolls and the guys managed to each bring a 2nd one with them to eat. Me, I bought an ice cream bar. This calls for a celebration.

Chapter 15

Rose asks what they expect to have supplied in exchange for working. Roman tells her he is retired and tired. Tired of living in town with nothing to do. Thad wants to spend the summer with his Dad and also, out of town. He is tired of the women wanting to go bar hopping as their idea of fun.

Noah has just finished up his job and no plans made for getting another any time soon. He took the job thinking it would be a nice way to meet folks out along the road system and decide where he would like to settle down and build. Seems as soon as the local folk heard he was from the government, most were less than polite, so that idea wasn't so great.

All 3 guys wanted an out of town Alaskan experience. Rose said if they really did, they could start by building themselves a place to stay. She said she didn't have money, she had land and they were welcome to stay on some of it, as long as they were willing to sign a lease and go by her not allowing alcohol or drugs on the place.

Noah asked if he could continue staying in his camper on my place at present and maybe help out now and then, also, on both places.

"I guess, although it will be pretty cold come Winter."

He says by then, his Dad and brother should have a cozy place ready, if he comes and helps out a lot every day or so. His brother smacks him and says they won't need his help, they are big strong capable men that know how to do stuff, except maybe cook well. Of course Noah smacks him back and soon they were being overaged boys, trying to get the best hold. When their Dad said 'Boys' in that tone of voice, we knew it was something they had heard often in their life and they both instantly stopped. Yes, it looks like they were raised right.

Roman and Thad will stay in Roman's trailer tonight and then see what needs done to build a nice small place for them to live a while.

Noah comes back to his camper on my place. "I hope you don't mind, I enjoy staying here and we work well together, I think." he says.

I have to agree. Besides being nice to look at, he is a lot of help and pleasant company. Without his help, it would have taken me a lot longer to get the firewood and woodshed done. Plus the help from Will and Shari really put me ahead of my self-imposed schedule for summer jobs on my place.

I feel bad for Will and Shari, having yet another body show up on their place. I don't know if they will want to stay in their house yet or not. However, this time, it should not be of interest to the Troopers as nothing pointed to it being involved and they already had all the evidence they had taken when there the last time.

The next day, I go on over to see Rose and Kara. As we talk, I ask if they have all the firewood in that they will need for the coming winter. Rose says she is working on enough for another winter, besides, just in

case she can't get out and do it. Kara still has a little
bit left to get for a years supply and would like to
finally build her woodshed. I suggest we all come
work here a few days to get the immediate jobs done
and then go help Will and Shari get their place ready
for winter. They have never wintered here and no idea
of what to get done. With only the 2 of them and her
pregnant, it could be hard on them. Rose and Kara
exchange looks and agree. Since we have extra help,
we can make use of it. We talk a bit more and decide
to see if the men have decided what they want to build
and if they would like assistance on it as part of the
jobs to do here.

   We all head over to the trailer where they are staying
and soon we are walking around and looking the area
over. Since the trailer is parked in an out of the way
area on the old roadbed and it is as compacted as a
person could wish for, for building pad, they ask if it is
okay to build right there. It would simplify snow
removal, also. Rose and Kara snickered and I knew I
would have to find out later, why.

   Roman liked the shop Rose had built below her
house, so they were going for simple, and easy, like it is.
They did decide to use 2x6's instead of 2x4s for the
walls like Rose had. She said she would have, too, if
she had the money at the time. It is 16'x24' and 2
story with both stories open and no interior walls to
block space. Plenty of room for 2 people to be
comfortable as Kara had lived in the shop 2 winters
with 3 teenagers, 2 dogs and 8 cats and they all
survived it.

   The guys drew up a material list and headed in to

town to pick up at least enough to start the project.

Rose, Kara and I decided to all head over to see how Will and Shari were making out. Also to see if our idea on lending a hand was okay.

Shari was out in the greenhouse when we pulled in. Will was out behind it, weeding a bit in the garden near the greenhouse. They both were wearing handguns which we had all suggested to them a while back. A rifle or shotgun is effective, but hard to carry while working. If you have set it down somewhere while working, it isn't going to do you any good when you need it in a hurry.

They both looked like they could use a break, so our visit wasn't too much of an interruption. Shari was having a time with morning sickness and looked a bit peaked. She wanted to learn to sew, so Rose offered to show her how. Hmm, maybe I should sit in. I knew how to sew furs, but not so well on material. Rose said she could show us how to darn socks even, if we were so inclined. Well, maybe. I do have some that could use a bit of help.

Will and Shari were happy to hear our suggestion and offered to come help on Rose and Kara's projects first, but we said if they wanted to help the guys on the cabin, that maybe half a day instead of taking them from their projects all day. They had helped so much on mine and were far behind on their own stuff. Besides, they had helped on the water project at Rose's.

As we were pulling back onto the road, Roman's truck came by. Wow, that was one quick trip to town and it was loaded with building supplies. Those men wanted to get building.

We followed them into the driveway and all pitched in to help unload. Rose had some old pallets sitting over beside the shack, so we stacked boards up off the ground on the pallets.

It did not take long to square out the corners and place the pier blocks they were using for supports. Rose and Kara came back in a few minutes wearing tool belts and I grabbed mine out of the back of my truck. In no time at all, we had the floor laid out and nailed and set on the pier blocks the guys had set in a grid inside the squared area. Roman had bought wire mesh to put under to keep squirrels out of the insulation, so we placed that and nailed it before nailing the 3 sections of flooring in place. We have build it in 3 8'x16' sections and would nail them together for the 16'x24' floor. After we had the floor in place, we filled the sections with insulation, then started nailing on the plywood sub floor. In just a few minutes, we had that done, too. Wow, this should go fast with all of us working on it.

Roman had picked up a few windows but not as many as he would need for the whole project. He decided where he would like them to be and marked it on the edges of the floor. Then we started on the walls. He had bought T 1-11 siding for the outside, so as we made a section of wall, we placed the window, covered with house wrap, taped, cut the siding needed and covered the wall, then stood it up and nailed. We had the 4 walls done before we all took a break. It looked like a house already.

Kara stopped a bit after we got started to open the shack. She came over with to-go boxes and gave us lunch.   When Roman tried to pay her, she said it was just stuff that hadn't been selling well and she would rather it was used then feed it to the birds or let it spoil. Later, he left a good tip in her tip jar.

After we ate, we built 2 of the upstairs floor sections, by laying them out on the bottom floor and then after assembling them, lifting them up and someone up on a ladder pulling, we got them into position and nailed the sections on both ends of the building.   After building a small section of wall, near an outside wall for the staircase to go up, we would use joist hangers to build the center section of the upstairs floor.   That small 8 foot section of wall was simple and placed about 3 feet out from the wall for a nice wide staircase.   Rose marked out the stair stringers on the 2"x12" boards and Noah cut them out. He nailed 3 foot long 2x4s spaced along them to hold them in place and then placed inside the short wall.   We moved the wall a bit to get a snug fit and nailed it all into place. Now, we could go up and down the stairs if we walked carefully on the edges of the stringers.   Thad came over with some 3 foot boards and tacked them in place up the stairs so we didn't have to go tippytoeing on the stringers.   Not fancy, but it worked.

Roman got out the joist hangers and we got to work upstairs after placing a couple sheets of plywood down across the floor joists so it would be easier to work. As soon as we had the joist hangers fastened on, the joists were placed and nailed in and the plywood sub floor was handed up and nailed down.   Rose was darn good at trimming it even with a chainsaw.   She said she did have some experience at it.   We were actually ready to start the upstairs walls.

Roman was almost in shock. He didn't have the windows or enough T 1-11 for the upstairs. He was going to have to make another trip to town. The building supply store doesn't close until 10 pm, so he would just go again this evening. He thought he better pick up some more nails also, since we tend to use a lot, if 1 is good, 3 are better.

I said good-bye and headed for home. Noah was going to ride in with his Dad and Thad was going to stay and go cut firewood for Kara. I think he likes her.

Chapter 16

After I get home, I feed my chicks that are looking long and leggy now. The little roosters are trying to crow once in a while and sound funny. I hurry and pick a bunch of small weeds from the garden and bring them over to dump in the pen for them. Then I check out how the ice house is looking and if I need more gravel. It seems to be firming up nicely as it dries so maybe it will be fine.

I start up the tiller and run it between the rows quickly to make the garden look better and not let the weeds get too good a start on me. I use the rake on the sides of the hills so all that is left is the actual rows on top of each hill to pull weeds out of and I have been keeping them pulled fairly well for the chicks.

After I go in the house, I reheat some leftovers and eat as I sort through laundry needing folded. I figured I would have it all ready to need washed again if I waited long enough to fold it. Certainly was working out that way, right now. I tossed all the underwear and socks into a basket and did fold the T shirts and pants. A pair of the Carhardt pants for working in tomorrow and a long sleeved T shirt would work well. It is my standard day to day wear. T shirt color changes and sometimes the pants, too, depending on which pair gets worn. I dress for comfort while I work, not for anyone's fashion sense. A pair of athletic shoes finishes the outfit. I'm set for tomorrow. We can probably have the cabin ready for a roof by tomorrow evening. That part I will be willing to leave to the guys.

I'm up early the next morning and have transplanted a few more shrubs around the new ice house. It is starting to look like it has been there a while and blending in with the surroundings rather well. The moss and bushes in the surface I had cut out in chunks has apparently not suffered too much and is growing right back.

As I walk over to the woodshed, Pal presses against my leg and a low growl rumbles through him. I stop nad look around, trying to see what is bothering him. Pretty soon he relaxes and we continue walking to the woodshed. Now he has me feeling jumpy, so when Noah walks around the corner of the woodshed a bit later, I nearly jump out of my shoes.

"Oh, I'm sorry, didn't mean to scare you." he says as he steps into the shed.

"Well, it wasn't exactly you that scared me. Pal was growling at something out back here and then you said hi and I wasn't expecting it." I reply.

He is suddenly all business, "What did you see and did you hear anything?"

"Not really, maybe some brush crackling on down over the bank. I'm not sure." I don't feel too secure and am happy to have Pal and Noah both staying here.

He asks if he should move his camper up to my yard and right now, that sounds pretty good. So I say sure.

After the camper is loaded and moved up the hill to my yard we leave it on the truck and use mine to go over to help on his Dad's cabin. Odd, when Roman and Thad will both be living in it and are both paying for the materials, we all call it Roman's cabin.

We unload Roman's pickup and start loading stuff up onto the 2nd floor for the walls. In short order, we are in production again and walls are being built. Rose had us leave the siding stick up and cut slots wide enough for the rafters every 2 feet. We taped the wrap to the top of each piece to hold it in place until the rafters were on. This gave the top of the side walls the appearance of arrow slots. The side walls were the short sides of the cabin and only 6 feet high. The gable ends were across the long section and went up to 12 feet at the top of the point. This gave more heigth and more light into the upstairs room and a good pitch to the roof for snow to slide off. The ridge beam would be shorter, too. 20 feet instead of 28 feet. Much lighter for us to place after the walls were all up. We assembled the beam across the floor on the second floor, using 2" x 12"s, liquid nails and strips of plywood between another 2"x12". The beam was 3 2"x12"s wide   Rose cut the ends slightly tapered so they would look finished.   I had brought my ladders and Rose and Kara had ladders, so did Roman, in his trailer, so we had plenty of ladders for everyone to be able to walk the beam up the ladders and slide into it's slot on each end.   Even with all of us it was still heavy and awkward but we didn't drop it.   We did almost put it in upside down, but caught that mistake seconds before it became reality.   Kara said they had actually done that on one of hers.   Very difficult to lift back up out of the slots and turn, once it is in.

The top plates are nailed on the side walls and it is

ready to start putting up rafters.   For a crew of amateurs, we are doing pretty darn good.

We load the rafters up to the 2nd floor and wish we had done it when we loaded the wall material as it would have been much easier, even if we had to keep moving it out of our way as we worked.   Rose marked out where to cut the birds mouths and lined them up with that side up, walked down them with her chainsaw and made the first cut on all of them at once.   Then a slight notch where the angle cut started to finish.   As each rafter was turned on its side, she cut from the notch to the end of the other cut and had the birds mouths cut.   The notches to fasten the outside rafters to the inside rafters were cut with the chainsaw also. The lower ends would rest on the top plate extensions we had made.   But a little extra support never hurts. With such a small cabin, putting the rafters on didn't take much time.   We crisscrossed them over the ridge beam and nailed them together.   There were only small pieces sticking out to be trimmed off and the chainsaw again worked very well for that.   Two of us on ladders started on fastening the house wrap over the rafters. We overlapped the walls a small amount, then cut and taped the wrap down in to the wrap left up from the wall.   A 1x2 tacked on top the 2x12 rafter held the house wrap firmly in place.   Then we moved on to the next rafter and repeated the operation.   This cabin would be water resistant by the time we were done and not a drop of rain hit the inside to dampen the insulation in the floor.

The wrap on top of the rafters with the 1x2's on top, will keep the insulation from poofing up and touching the roof, and making it a hot roof with ice buildup in winter. Any space at all between the insulation and the metal roof will allow air circulation and make it a cold roof.

As we wrapped the rafters, the guys were placing nailer strips over the 1x2's on the rafters, from ladders against the walls. It looks like Roman bought 1x6's to use to fasten the roofing to. We made a box and fastened it between the rafters to hold the chimney and for the guys to see where to go around with the nailers. We taped the house wrap down inside it and hoped no rain would enter before a chimney was added.

Kara opened the shack at noon and I headed down to see how Will and Shari were doing. As I started out the driveway, they were pulling in. They had come to help on the cabin. Oops, well, they were surprised.

Will asked Roman to mark out where he wanted electric lines and he would put them in for him. Roman went around the walls, marking for outlets and switches for overhead lights with magic marker.

Shari apologized for their being late, she had been barfing up the last years worth of food, she thought and wondered how anyone gained weight when pregnant if this lasted very long.

Shari and I pulled wire as Will drilled holes and placed outlet boxes. As soon as she knew what to do, I went back up and started on helping upstairs.

I tied a nail to a string and tacked it to the upper edge of the chimney box in the roof. Where it hit the floor would be where the hole would need cut for the chimney to come up from downstairs. I sure hope it is between floor joists. Well, it only needs a little bit of adjusting and it will be fine.   I draw the outline in magic marker where they will need to cut to put the insulated pipe support piece.

Then Rose and I start on installing the doors. Roman has bought 2 very nice metal clad insulated doors with a window in it.   Wow, I have never worked with a new door before.   We only have to shim in a couple of spots and it slides right in.   We have them screwed in place before the guys even notice what we were doing.   Then they yell a little bit that it was too heavy for us to be lifting.   Well, fiddle, it is in, isn't it? Guys.   Rose and I grin at each other and just keep on working.   It is kind of nice to have guys actually want to do the heavy stuff.

It is a large step up into the cabin, at the front door, so Rose and I bring over a large heavy duty pallet and place it on some flat stones and level it out.   Then we add a couple of boards so it only has narrow spaces between boards so no one will go between boards on their way in.   When Roman comes around the corner, he thanks us and says he would like to build an entryway porch later, to have a place to hang coats and to cut the wind coming in the door when going in or out of the house.

He has several sheets of T 1-11 siding left over and offers to put it on the outside of the shop Rose has, down the hill as she has never been able to side her shop.   Some of the extra house wrap to go under it, too.   She is speechless and almost tears up a bit, but then says yes, that would be wonderful.   He pulls out 3 sheets to use for his porch and the rest he loads back on his pickup.   He says with the trim left from the window cutouts and the walls, he will have plenty for a nice porch now.

Rose, Kara and I will leave the rest of the cabin work to the guys as they don't seem to mind being on ladders or roofs. With the house wrap over the rafters, the roof will shed light rain and should be okay inside until they can get the roof on. Rose had requested metal roofing as it is pretty much a lifetime roof and fire proof, also. It has a steep enough pitch to shed snow fairly well, also. No one should ever have to get back on it.

Rose and I walk over to the shack and talk to Kara a bit. Rose tells her the guys are going to put the leftover T 1-11 siding on the shop for her. We all just stand there, thinking of the difference in people. These 3 men not only said they would do something, they actually got right in and did it. Sometimes they didn't even say anything, they just stepped right up and started helping.

Rose says the spring is still running very well, even with the dry weather we have been having. She has been able to water the gardens and greenhouses from it and most of the laundry, too. She said it tastes good, also, although she didn't have it tested. Mine has been doing very well. Shari comes over about that time and she is happy with the small spring they have, too. She said they were digging a small ditch bringing it closer to the house and garden. She was planting wild rose bushes all around the edges of the clearing their house was in. She loved the flowers and wanted to make rosehip jelly and catsup. I think that is a very good idea and I will be planting more around my place, too.

Maybe similar to a hedge, even. Some raspberry plants here and there with the rose bushes. Good things to eat and a nice stickery hedge. No down side to that.

Will and Roman flip for who gets to buy us all dinner. Thad says it isn't too fair to Kara as she still has to fix it for us. She laughs and says she certainly doesn't mind and what would we all like to eat?

We each place our orders and she starts preparing our meals. I could get used to this and very spoiled. I have eaten out more often in the last month than I have in the last several years.

While we are eating, we talk about the next project needing done. Kara needs a woodshed which to me is the most important and then we need to fill it. Will and Shari also need a bigger woodshed and it filled. Rose has most of her woodshed filled, but another stack or two would be good, just to have on hand. I don't think it is possible to have too much on hand. Also, Roman and Thad should have a woodshed and firewood if they are planning on staying.

Roman plans on another trip to town tomorrow morning, early, for materials to finish up the cabin. Insulation, foam board, vapor barrier and plywood. Some light fixtures and electrical outlets, maybe some plumbing stuff, too. He asked if any of us needed anything from town. No one did, so we all said good evening and headed our separate ways.

Chapter 17

I started my rose transplanting the next morning when I got up.   There were small plants all over my place so I dug and moved them into a triple row line around my yard.   I was afraid it might be too late in summer to fertilize them much, so just made sure they were in good top soil in each planting hole I dug.   I still had a few buckets of the dirt from the ice house that was nice rich looking soil and I added some ashes and sand to it in each hole.   The raspberry plants I placed along the outside row of the 3 rows planted. As I could afford it, I wanted to add some rugosa roses to the rows, also.   They had wicked thorns but large rosehips for vitamin C and would make excellent tea, besides the jelly and catsup.   I had assorted stickers to show for my efforts by the time Noah showed up for us to go work on Kara's woodshed.

Since he was driving today, I picked and pulled thorns on the way over.   Since Kara was working the shack, we just went ahead and started her woodshed. She had supplies from other projects around and we had brought a few items, so we set up the pier blocks where we thought would be a good area and then the posts on them.   Once the first corner was built, it was much easier to get the rest up and fastened together.

We had a good start by the time Roman and Thad got back from town and they were so proud of themselves, they had found a deal on a nice car haul trailer and bought it.   They had it piled high with all the stuff they had managed to get in such a short time. The trailer was backed over beside Roman's shop trailer and it looked like he was set to go into business.

With Roman, Thad, Rose, Noah and I working on the woodshed, we soon had the rough frame done. All it needed was a few more cross braces and then we decided to fix it up like mine and add another side to it and double her space.

By the time we stopped, that evening, she had the frame for a nice very large woodshed in her yard. Tomorrow, we would start on rafters for it and the guys would probably roof the cabin so the interior didn't get any stray showers if it decided to rain.

When Kara came down, she just stood there and looked. Then she said that she had about given up ever having one after all the years she had lived there without and fought with digging her firewood out from under deep snow most of the winter. She said she realized temper did warm a person up, but thought the blood pressure issue offset the gain.

The next morning, the guys got right to work on the roof of the little cabin and had it done, complete with chimney jack, by noon. Then they came down and put the rest of the rafter poles on the woodshed. Rose and I had quite a pile set out to use and had placed a few after we nailed in more cross bracing. We had it looking very nice and it seemed sturdy enough for all of us to be on the roof, if we so desired, which she and I didn't. Neither of us are fans of high places. Even not very high places. She has no sense of balance left after a few accidents and I am just chicken.

We crisscrossed the poles at the peak and nailed them in place, leaving the ends hang. We could cut them off later, when we saw how much the metal roof would cover. We also made a 4 foot wide doorway in the end closest to the house. It would be easier packing firewood through a wide doorway or, if she got a 4 wheeler or snow machine, she could store it inside if she wished.

Roman brought down a bundle of roughcut 2x4s he had bought very cheaply in town, and we used them as nailer boards across the poles to fasten the metal roofing to.

I asked Rose where they were getting their firewood from. She said they had a permit to get a certain amount from the old firebreak she had cut years before along the bottom of her property. We decided I would go down with her and Kara in the morning and cut firewood while the guys roofed the woodshed.

The next morning, we headed down the hill on a road she had built when she first bought the property. Once we got to the end of it, the firebreak was obvious. She had done quite a job with the old dozer. We cut and loaded firewood all morning until shortly before noon. Then Kara had to go change and open the shack. We had both pickups overloaded and a very large pile ready to haul. So we all went up the hill with the pickup loads.

The guys were just coming off the roof and Roman asked if we had any ridge cap around. None of us did, so he cut a sheet of roofing into thirds the long way and bowed it over the ridge and screwed it on. It looked pretty darn good to me. We unloaded the firewood and went back for more. Noah and Thad came with us and Roman started on the rest of the ridge caps he was making. The rest of the wood we had cut was loaded and back up and unloaded in record time.   The pile of wood getting pitched in through the door was looking good, but I knew as soon as it was actually stacked, it wasn't all that much wood.

We dragged the rest of the poles we had stacked for building, inside.   Kara had some chunks of old rug out back, so we put the rug down first, and laid a double row of poles out to put the cut firewood on to keep it off the ground. Then started stacking firewood.   The woodshed was large enough for about 2 years worth of firewood, so it was going to take quite a while to make any good showing on filling it up.   We had more cut down and ready to cut to lengths, but it could wait a while.   Like tomorrow or maybe another day.

Rose and I thought we should go build a shed for Will and Shari next, then take turns cutting wood for each place.   After their shed, we could fix one up by the new cabin for Roman and his sons.   This could be the summer of the woodshed.   It was certainly something we all needed done.

The next morning, we loaded some peeled logs for uprights and headed over to Will and Shari's.   They were surprised to see us as they had not made it over yesterday.   Shari was having a very hard time with her morning sickness and Will didn't want to leave her. We could understand that and hoped she got over that part sooner rather than later on.

Will showed us where he would like a woodshed to be and we got started.   We were getting this down to a science on laying out and building.   Soon we had the first post up and then another with a brace between them.   Then one at an angle and the first corner was up and stabilizing the whole thing a bit.   10 ft. x 24 ft.

seemed a good size as they already had a smaller shed. So we went ahead and made this one a single shed type building. They could always add another side on it later, like mine was and have more room. This place, being an older established site, had a good supply of discarded and salvaged materials out back, like any good Alaskan home. So we went scrounging for nailer boards and roofing and found both. Will took his little 4 wheeler ATV and trailer over and loaded all the stuff and brought it back. Shari managed to fix a nice lunch for everyone although she was still pretty green around the edges herself and didn't eat.

By late afternoon, we had a nice woodshed for them, now all they needed was wood to fill it. Will had been cutting and filling the old shed, so they were doing well. If he got that shed filled and this one, he would have a large margin for bad weather or illness, not being able to go cut wood for a while.

We headed back to Rose and Kara's to drop off the items we had brought from there. Then Noah took me home. He went back to help his Dad and brother on the cabin, I had work to catch up on here at home.

Late that evening, I heard a vehicle pull in. It didn't sound like Noah, so I went to check and here came Roman pulling his new trailer. But he had made sides for it and it was loaded with logs. He pulled over near my woodshed and his sons jumped out and started unloading. He came over and asked how I was doing and I said "Fine, but I thought everyone else needed firewood more than I do."

He said "Yes, they all need it, and they each got a load tonight. I found a guy down near the river clearing his plot of ground and planning on burning all these nice trees. So the boys and I made him a deal. We will haul away all the trees for him so he don't have to burn them."

"What? He was going to burn them? Doesn't he think he is going to need firewood?"

Roman nodded and replied "No, he plans on only burning oil or propane and not smelly wood."

Oh my, another one of those guys. Just what we needed in the area although he is supplying us with firewood. Although, as I check this load of wood, I notice it is almost all spruce and in 8 foot lengths. I think these would be best peeled and used for building. I mention this to Roman and he said he had thought so also, and that is why I got the load of spruce when most of the others got birch, except Rose. She also got a load of spruce.

The trailer load is probably close to 3 cords and the load in the pickup is just under a cord, since he has a heavy duty 1 ton beefed up a lot. He said it really speeded up the wood getting as this was all cut and piled already, he and the boys had just loaded it and delivered.

About then, I remembered my bread in the oven and ran to check. Sure enough, the bread looked golden brown and the cinnamon rolls were just ready to pull out and serve. Evidently, the guys thought so too, as there was a tap on the door and I yelled come in, as I pulled them out onto the counter.

There is just something about the odor of fresh out of the oven cinnamon rolls that acts like an irresistible attractant to noses. The guys file in sniffing the air as they head to the counter. I turn the pan over and dump the rolls onto a cookie sheet. Plates, forks and butter on the counter and soon the guys are contently scorching their mouths on molten hot sugar/cinnamon and bread. I fill glasses with cold water and set them close to each man. These guys appreciate fresh rolls.

One of these days I will make an extra special potato recipe I sometimes make when I have a lot of time and supplies on hand. These are just regular bread dough recipe.

I put one on a paper towel and go to check on the chicks and greenhouse. I go to the greenhouse first and open the end doors for fresh air to move through the building. It is warm enough even all night, to leave it open. I set my roll down, as for me they are still a bit too warm to eat and go check on the plants to see if I need to water in the morning. I pull a few weeds in among the plants and start back to the house. Then remember the roll I left by the other door so go back for it but can't find it, the paper towel is there, so a Jay must have sneaked in and grabbed it. I was busy long enough the Jay could have taken the whole thing off. Maybe the guys have left one for me in the house.

When I go back in, they are all sitting around the table looking relaxed and very full. Yes, they did leave me one on the cookie sheet. I eat it and they are almost asleep in their seats. It has been a long hard few days for them and they need the rest, but would be more comfortable on the couch. I suggest this and they seem to rouse a bit and then stumble over to the couch. I tell them, if they want, they can spend the night in the little old cabin Will and Shari had stayed in a while back and Noah has his camper in the yard. They nod sleepily and head out the door to use the cabin and camper. I clean up a bit and head for bed.

I am up early so start a good sized breakfast as the pickup and trailer are still in my yard. I have potatoes frying and bear ham cooking in the oven and eggs ready to fry when the first signs of life show up at the cabin. Then Roman and Thad come out the door and pound on Noah's door. He comes out looking very good indeed. I meet them at the door and ask how they like their eggs. Roman says I am a goddess and his sons agree. I figure the rolls were probably their evening meal yesterday so they must be starving this morning and have cooked quantities to match. I put the slices of buttered bread on the griddle and fix their eggs, just as the bear ham comes out of the oven. The food is dished up and on the table as they come over and sit at the table. I tried my hand at making a pot of coffee and they each drank a cup, but no one asked for seconds. Coffee is something I need to practice on, I guess. I drink tea or chocolate, so it has not been a priority.

They do justice to the food, though. As hard as they have been working, it is no wonder. After breakfast, they are going back to see if the guy has any more trees to clear off. After he builds, he will probably spend a fortune planting trees to replace what he cut down and have to wait all his life for them to grow big enough to matter.

I grab some of the toasted bread slices in a paper towel and head over to the old cabin to make sure I have it clean and ready for the next house guests that need a place to stay. The guys had folded up the used sheets and placed them near the door and made the bed with clean sheets from the shelf by the bed. What thoughtful guys, they had very good mothers.

I take the sheets over to the washer which is set up outside for the summer and start the little generator. I fill the washer with buckets of water and the sheets and while it washes, bring out my laundry, also. By the time this load is done, I have the start of weeding on this corner of the garden and after hanging the sheets, put in my work clothes. I weed some more in the garden and run the tiller around between the rows. The potatoes need hilling, so I start on that. As I hang the load of work clothes and have my sheets and underwear in the last load, the guys pull in yet again, with another load. They unload and ask if they bring laundry, if I would do it for them? I say sure, once in a while I can do that. Another load now and then won't make any difference. Noah heads to his camper and brings out a bag of laundry. My load is ready to add the next buckets of water for rinse, and then his will go in. Now that I have the water from the spring, I can do extras. Since we haven't had rain in a while, my rainwater system would have ran out quite a while back, but I keep refilling the tank for showers from the spring.

They have already hauled loads to each of the other places again, before bringing me another load of spruce. I plan on setting up the sawhorses and getting out the drawknife and peeling most of these for building projects. I think there are enough. Maybe a small barn. Hmmmm, more projects.

They think maybe there will be at least one more load per place tomorrow and then not much else from down the road, but this is an amazing amount of wood in a very short time. I better go help Rose and Kara cut theirs to length, if they are using it for firewood.

When I mention this, Roman says he thinks Rose is peeling hers, if so, he will help her and that Thad is cutting Kara's up for her. Okay, so I will work on mine.

The laundry is ready for rinse, so I add the water and it goes back to rinsing. We talk a little bit and then the guys head back over to work on the cabin. Roman was working on Rose's backhoe and asked if he could dig an outhouse hole for the cabin, so that was his project for the evening. The washer quits and I turn off the generator and hang the clothes.

I hill the rest of the potatoes and go inside to rest and figure what I am going to fix for dinner. The bear has just about been used up. It has certainly been handy to have on hand or I would have been feeding everyone vegetarian meals.

I see an Arctic hare in the garden and grab the .22. Maybe dinner won't be a problem. I get a head shot and go pick up dinner and skin and clean it. I think maybe stir fry with rice would be good, so debone the hare and put the meat to soak in some cold water with a bit of baking soda in it. There are probably enough pea pods ready to pick in the garden and I have onions to slice thin. After picking the peas, and cleaning them, I drain the meat and make a marinade of soy sauce, ginger and garlic to soak it in until time to cook. I have it cut into small bite sized slices and put it and the marinade in a zipper type baggie.

I tack the hide to the wall inside the woodshed to dry.

Will and Shari pull in as I am starting a pot of rice. So I add another cupful to the pot. Then Roman, Thad and Noah show up, so I pull out a bigger pot and add more rice and water. I can add more sliced onion to the stir fry. I slice the pea pods smaller than usual, too. Maybe make lots of sauce.

They are all still out on the yard talking and the rice has come to a boil and been turned down, the pan is sizzling for the stir fry and I need to figure a bit more to add to it all. I find one of the last heads of cabbage from the ones I bought in the early Spring. The outer leaves are shriveled, but the heart is still firm and good, so I slice it thin and add to the pile for the stir fry. I add the meat and stir it quickly and pull over to the side, then add the vegetables and stir some more, then set the pan off the stove a minute while adding some more soy sauce and cornstarch to the marinade left in the baggie. I put the pan back over the heat and add the sauce, stirring continuously. It thickens up nicely and I add a bit more water, not supposed to be that thick. I set the pot of rice on the counter and the pan of stir fry, then start dishing it up like an assembly line as they come in the door. Since there is limited topping, I dish it up. A pile of rice and the stir fry on top, with soy sauce and sliced ginger on the table and chopsticks in a glass also, if they prefer. I dig out a tube of wasabi paste and put it on the table, also.

Everyone seems to be enjoying it, even Shari and she was surprised. I think it is mostly that she didn't have to smell it cooking before trying to eat it. She is careful to not overdo and eats a small amount, waits a bit and a little bit more. I had fixed her a small plate full, anyway. I think everyone thinks it is chicken. Oh well, not going to say anything now. Never mentioned bear, why mention little cute bunny. No one has mentioned any religious reasons not to eat any so other than that, I won't volunteer what they are eating here.

Shari wants to get some chickens like I have. She enjoys fresh eggs and was used to having them at home. I think it may be too late in the season to find chicks, but suggest they try the feed stores in town when they go in next time.

I would like to build a small barn and maybe have a couple of goats and maybe some rabbits, but not sure how much I could grow, for feed for them and if I have to buy it all, that probably won't save much money.

Roman says Rose is thinking of the same thing, maybe having a couple of goats to have milk to make cheese. He says she has a problem killing something after she has raised it. Sort of strange for a hunter, but she says she has to look at game animals as steaks, roasts and burger, then she can shoot them. But something she has cuddled and held as cute little babies is another story. Well, I can see that. I have some of the chicks I have been raising that are so friendly and cute and come snuggle next to me when I sit on the step. I really doubt if I could kill one of them very easily, either. A good thing I want them for eggs. Grouse and Ptarmigan will be my chicken dinners.

Chapter 18

After dinner, we sit around talking about the small community we seem to be making, here. Yes, we are spread out quite a bit, but it is still a community of sorts. There are other people living a bit farther away from us, but not many of them. We talk about meeting them, but decide it would be better to include Rose and Kara in that discussion.

Everyone finally decides it is time to get some sleep, and we all go our separate ways. The long daylight hours make it hard to realize we have talked half the night away.

The next morning, I head over to see Rose after getting my chores done around the place and refilling my water tank for showers and laundry. I love that spring.

She is up at the cabin the guys are building, so we go check how they are progressing. They have a woodstove set up in the downstairs room and pipe out the roof. They could stay in here if they needed to, before cold weather. Roman has put laminate flooring down, on both floors. This is going to be a very nice little cabin. The guys have most of the insulation in and are working on putting the foil faced foam board up over the fiberglas insulation. It makes a thermal break so heat doesn't transfer out at each stud and rafter. They have taped the foam board seams, also. Then a good vapor barrier over that, with the seams taped and taped around the electrical outlets also. They cut small pieces of the foam board to place inside each outlet box and have caulked where the wire comes through to cut heat loss, ice buildup and drafts. The guys are following Rose's building pattern that she used for the houses built here. It seems to work well. They have large homes and very easy to heat. This little cabin should be easy to heat and very comfortable, no matter what the weather.

They are fixing a small shower stall and toilet under the staircase and to the other wall. The door will open from the kitchen area. Roman dug an outhouse hole just behind the cabin, and is piping the bathroom directly into it. They will have a kitchen sink with a pipe running into it, also. He will place a vent pipe up the back of the outhouse to near the roof of the house, for odors. This is going to be one very nice little cabin. Amazing what you can do if you have a little bit of money and can buy new.

Kara comes up to open the shack and we all go over and take up the discussion from last night at my house. Will and Shari pulled in about that time, so that was perfect.

Some customers pull in and Kara is busy for a bit, so we wait until she is free again to start. Shari actually starts the conversation about us being a community. That girl is getting some backbone out here. When she finishes, Roman says a few words, then Will chips in and Noah. Rose and Kara take it all in and think it over. They agree that we are a loosely knit community and maybe we should start meeting others in the area. Kara says some have been coming in to buy meals and cigarettes. So she can talk to them a bit more. Some are very much out here to be left alone. She was on pretty good terms with most, as they knew she also did not welcome visitors to just stop on a whim, if she didn't know them.

Lots of people were curious about the houses here and the whole area, but most actually did pay attention to the road signs and word did get around after Kara shot over the heads of some guys that were determined to use the driveway for access to the property on down the hill from here.   Kara got a lot of business from folks that were just plain curious about what was in here.   Why on earth the State decided on making remote parcel staking available near here, I will never know.   There really is no access to it.   So Rose and Kara get to deal with a bunch of jerks.   The guys coming out to stake weren't so great, either.

Kara says she will mention to the other folk in the area as they stop in, about us all being a bit more of a community for helping each other if in need or someone injured.   One fellow had almost froze last winter as he fell and broke his ankle and couldn't get firewood in very well.   He had crawled in and out, dragging one piece at a time, every day and his ankle still wasn't too good.   It had healed solid, so didn't bend now.   We wondered if we should haul a load of firewood over and drop it off at his house, just as a hello and sorry he wasn't doing so great.

Noah drove down to the river to see if the guy clearing his lot had more trees to get rid of, and he had about another trailer load.   So the guys went down and loaded it up.   Rose rode along with the guys to deliver it, as she knew where the man lived and had spoken to him a couple of times.   Kara sent a sandwich, the kind he had ordered, when he had stopped in a couple of times.

He lived just a short distance beyond my place, so I

followed them as far as my place and went home. Later, Noah told me the man was very surprised to see them and after Rose talked to him, he was okay with the delivery. The guys unloaded the logs and he said he could cut them up and he appreciated the thought, wasn't sure he wanted them to ever do it again though. Rose gave him the to-go box and they backed out and came home. Well, to Rose's place which for the time is their home too.

As nice as the little cabin is, that they are building, it looks like they could be settling in for a very long time. The guys head on in to town after dropping Rose off. They want to get more supplies to finish up the cabin and start stocking it a bit. It's a good thing the building supply store is open early in the morning and late into the evening, in summer. They hauled everyone's trash in, since they took the trailer, also.

When the guys come back, we know they have found the joys of visiting the transfer stations in Fairbanks. These are areas set aside, with roofs over them and concrete pad for folks to set out stuff that is too good to trash and not the time and energy to sell. They have found older cabinets they need for the kitchen and possibly a propane cook stove, with pilot light instead of electronic ignition, if it works. Those are hard to find for folks living way out with no electricity. They also had some used windows and doors on the trailer. Everything looked in excellent condition. I have found clothes folded and set out still warm from a dryer. Most of my carhartt pants are from there. I certainly can't afford to buy them.

They had managed to make it to the supply store

and had some nice light fixtures to hang in the cabin, a
sink and more sewer line, some counter top and some
totes they have filled with groceries.   On the very back
of the trailer, they have some polydrums of fuel.   We
need to get their woodshed built, so they have an area
to place those without water getting in them or anyone
seeing what they have on hand.

They had picked up some more of the pier blocks,
so we would start on their woodshed in the morning.
They laid out the size and set the pier blocks this
evening.   I will come over in the morning to help.

Noah is late getting to my place and telling me all
about this, as he is unloading some bags of groceries in
my kitchen.   I'm not sure what he is doing, but he
explains they have ate so much at my place, they felt
guilty, so wanted to replace some.   Knowing I don't
have electricity, they bought cans of dried storage
foods, which is great but expensive.   They did buy a
couple of 50 pound bags of flour and of sugar, also.
He said they really like the breads and cinnamon rolls.

I will save the cans of dried foods and continue
feeding them bear, hare and whatever else I manage to
kill around the area.   I would like to get some more of
those, could store them in the back of the ice house in
totes to keep them dry.   Maybe I should pan the creek
some more and see if I can afford to buy a supply.

Very early the next morning, I went down to the
little creek down the hill and panned a while.   It is hard
on my back, so I don't stay long.   I do find some color
and save it in a small bottle.   This is going to take
some time to earn enough for groceries and fuel.   I
need to pick up some more chains for my chainsaw,

spark plugs and bar oil.

By the time I get back to the house, it is time for breakfast and then over to build another woodshed. I stash the pan behind the seat in my pickup and heat up a bun for breakfast.

Noah shows up just as I have it ready to eat, so I run out the door with tool belt in one hand and hot toasted bun in the other. He asks if it is for him. Oh darn, I tear it in half and hand him half as I get in the truck. He looks slightly guilty but goes ahead and eats it.

We pull in as the rest are starting to place the first post. By now we have this down to a routine. This woodshed should go up very fast. By noon, we have it ready to roof. Noah goes over and buys me a sandwich to make up for eating half my breakfast. Well, maybe I will share better after this.

I visit with Kara while I eat. We talk a bit about getting supplies on hand. She thinks it is better to have extra of everything. Bad weather, anything, can make it difficult to restock and the last couple of years, the stores in Fairbanks are noted for being out of stock on a lot of items needed. It always comes in, but we don't go to town often enough to keep checking for new stock on the shelves. So she and Rose have been trying to keep as much on hand as possible and replacing anything as they use it. Sounds like a good idea to me. I think everyone out here is on limited income, one way or another, so we can't afford to just go to town even if we wanted to make that long trip every few days. At least all the locals or long term folk are.

Rose offers me a ride home so Noah can stay and help roof the woodshed and whatever other projects they need to do. They will probably go check and see if the guy has any more wood they can salvage. Later, I find they have gotten about a full load, but he is almost done.

Rose was interested in all I had built here. She had never been over here before. Most of us out here are private people and give others their privacy, also. She says great minds think alike as we have done a lot of similar things on our properties. She weeded as we walked through the gardens just like I was. It's hard not to do things you see needing done.

We went in the house and she liked my artwork, suggesting I come see some of hers, also. It is funny, we had never met, but had worked in a lot of the same fields. Guiding, taxidermy, mining and several others. She had been a Registered Guide, I, a 1st class Assistant. Whatever, it is hard work. That was what her place was supposed to have been. A hunting and aurora watching lodge. Her partners never coughed up the money and she spent every dime buying the land. So she refused to add their names on the title and another reason she makes everyone sign a lease.

Alaska has an Adverse Possession Law. After 7 years of claiming property, a person can advertise the owner out. A woman near here was being nice and allowed the folks with property beyond hers to cut across her land to reach theirs. They served her with Court papers to give them the Right to that strip of her land and she lost it. They had used it free for 7 years and never bothered to build the driveway that was platted, to theirs.   Then they sold their property and hers went with it, no longer hers and no Right to stop others from using it.   Really makes a person want to do good deeds.

After Rose left, I started a batch of bread dough. It seems to go quite fast.   I think I will make large buns and a loaf of bread.   The cinnamon rolls are a given.

As I am taking the rolls out of the oven, Noah and his Dad and brother pull in.   They are going looking for areas to cut firewood.   They figure maybe they can deal with some of the mine owners up the road, to clear the trees out of their way.   They immediately decide a short break is in order and have a cinnamon roll and one to go on.   A good thing these guys work hard or they might get fat here.

I stick a couple on a paper towel and go work in the greenhouse.   I must be losing it dreaming about lovely melted chocolate eyes, and ate one without even noticing, because when I go over to the paper towel, there is only one on it.   Unless the Jays are getting into the shelf in the greenhouse.   Or a squirrel.

I have a pot of stew on the stove from the remains of the bear.   It is getting pretty slim pickings.   I am glad I canned every bit, it has came in handy often this summer.   So when the guys pull back in to let me know how it went, they have dinner with me.   Stew and buns, filled with melted cheese.   Then another cinnamon roll for dessert.   I wonder if they will ever get tired of those.

I ride over to Rose's the next morning, to see if there are any projects needing attention.   I find Rose and Kara cutting up the firewood and stacking it in the woodshed.   They are also stacking the stack they had against the house over in the other half of the shed.

We work until shortly before noon, then Kara goes to get cleaned up and head up to open the shack.

Rose and I walk down to her house.   It is very large and nice looking.   She has a sun porch across the front and grows salad veggies on it in winter.   In winter, it is a large walk-in fridge, too.   Not very warm, so only cold weather crops survive most of the winter on it.   She transplants what she has late started, just for that.

I really like her artwork.   Most is in a soft black and white and portray animals and people, not many people.   Some oils and some pen and ink.

She also has published some books.   She says they are only self published, not like a publisher bought them and did it for her.   She says it is one way to earn a bit of extra money living way out here.   They have internet when the generators are on, she says if I have a laptop, I can bring it over at free time which is between 10 pm and 2 am.   The system doesn't work very well, but out here, it is nice, anyway.

Chapter 19

We walk back up the hill to the shack. Right after we get there, a rental SUV pulls into the turnaround area. A large hefty guy looking like a walking advertisement for a heart attack or stroke waiting to happen steps out and no other word for it, he moseys over. His thumbs hooked into his low slung belt. His belly hiding them quite well. He is trying to look like a good old boy that loves everyone but his eyes are hard and unsmiling, searching all around and missing very little. Just looking at the way he looks at Kara and Rose has my hackles rising. This is not a nice man. As soon as he opens his mouth, I groan inwardly.

"Why howdy do, little ladies."

Dang, another one of those but somehow I don't think I am going to change my first opinion on this one.

There are 2 other guys sitting in the SUV. They are watching every move being made and look like they would be more comfortable with shotguns in their hands. This looks like a hanging party to me. But Beer Gut is back to slathering it on thick.

"I don't suppose either of you little ladies know where I could find my dear daughter-in-law, would you? She done run off with some low life and is hiding, afraid to come back to her loving family. She thinks she might get a spanking and I am sure my son may reprimand her, but he loves that little gal."

Uh, he is talking about Shari. I saw the pictures of how he reprimanded her for nothing, and he would consider this more than nothing. Except he is dead and this man knows it. I ease over to where the guys are working and ask one of them to go warn Will and

Shari that her father-in-law is here.   He also has 2
more in his pack of wolves.   No, I am bad mouthing
wolves to lump them in together.   These are more like
hyenas.   Looking for weak and injured to gang up on
and tear to shreds.

I know this man knows his sons are dead, why is he
pretending they are not?   The Troopers would have
notified him back when they found Rod, and again
with tentative ID on Rob.

Rose and Kara are doing the same thing I did with
Will, the first time I met him.   They are acting like they
haven't a brain and why would anyone ever leave such a
nice family?   Rose has her hand clenched so tightly, I
think she is going to break something and soon.   I can
only imagine what Kara has in her hand, inside the
shack where she has a gun and knives.   I am wishing
for something to take care of Shari's problem, myself.

As we are standing there, wondering how we can
send this troll off on a wild goose chase, a Trooper
vehicle pulls in.   It is our friendly Trooper that has
been so nice about all the other problems.   He walks
over and asks the man for ID.   He shifts the man over
a bit so they can have a private conversation, but the
man isn't having any of it.   He is loud and blustering
and not about to back down.   The first thing I know,
he has swung a fist at the Trooper and somehow,
quicker than I was expecting, he is flat on his face on
the ground and the Trooper is cuffing him.   The other
two bail out of the SUV and run at the Troopers back
and Kara pulls up a nasty looking handgun and stops
them in their tracks by firing up into the air.   They
almost land on top the Trooper bent over their leader.

But they do get stopped. The Trooper stands up and brushes off the knees of his pants. When he turns to the "boys" the smile on his face seems to take the starch right out of them.

They haven't actually done anything, so he allows them to remain free while he manhandles the reluctant prisoner to his car. The man is screaming that he is a Sheriff and he will have the Troopers badge. The Trooper says that is fine, there are no Sheriffs in Alaska. He has always thought he would like to take up painting and tells him his number. Rose is snickering over behind the shack, Kara still has the gun in her hand, but down out of sight now. I have mine slid along my leg out of sight. Roman and Thad have managed to make it over near us and are standing with a gun each, also. The Trooper suggests to the Sheriff's buddies that they fly right back to where they came from and he better not hear of them causing any trouble for anyone. He does write down all their information from their ID and gives it back to them.

He does take the time to tell us that when they flew in and rented an SUV, the Troopers were notified and he had been following them. He had seen the pictures and read the report on Shari's condition after her loving family had taken such good care of her. All the healed up broken bones were listed, also.

Since the Sheriff had actually swung at the Trooper, he would be going straight to jail and held without bail as a flight risk.

As the Trooper in his car and the SUV are leaving the driveway, Will and Shari are pulling in with Noah. Shari has scrunched down so they cannot see her. We all explain what has happened. Will called the 2 buddies Beau and Luke and said they liked to think they were the epitome of the guys in the movies. He didn't think they would be dangerous without Royal in his capacity as Sheriff, backing them. Later, we learned that the 2 buddies had not flown out and were still hanging around in town. So now there was a buddy of Rod's and 2 buddies of his dad's still somewhere in the area. Just what we needed. But Will and Shari will certainly be careful and are getting a dog, too. They want one that is large enough for protection, but good natured to family. It would be an indoor dog except when out with them in the yard.

I suggested checking at the Pound. Sometimes can find well trained nice dogs there. They were planning on going in the next day, and would look.

Well, that certainly livened up our day. I would have missed that if I had stayed home and did my chores. Somehow, Rose managed to snap a picture, just as Royal swung at the Trooper and she has it ready to print out and send in with Will and Shari the next day. It will be pretty hard for Royal to say that never happened. I hope they keep him a very long time. Instead, they will probably send him home if he promises never to come back. Somehow, he doesn't seem the type to honor a promise he didn't want to make.

Chapter 20

Well, this has certainly been a lively afternoon. Will
and Shari come over as we are all putting our various

weapons away, Noah right behind them. Shari is nervously giggling and says she bets those guys never met women like us. "Let me guess, he started out by calling ya'll little ladies, right?"

Will looks sheepish at this and grins and pokes her. She is laughing outright by now. Rose goes over to her and says it will be okay. She says she does the same thing when scared half to death, she starts giggling and laughing. Shari is shaking so bad we find her a seat to sit down. Kara comes out with a sweater and puts it around her so she don't chill. She has been so afraid for so long, it is hitting her very hard. I just hope she doesn't let her guard down too soon. There are still 3 people not accounted for and who knows how long Royal will be held in jail?

I needn't have worried, she and Will both mention just that thing after a few minutes of relaxing. But at least now we have faces to the fear and knowing what is going on.

Will gets ice cream from Kara and hands it out to us. A little sugar may help Shari right now and the rest of us always like ice cream.

I ride back over to Will and Shari's and we work out in the garden a while, as we talk. They want to get their place a bit more secure. They do have a nice open area around the house and outbuildings so they can see if anyone is coming in. I suggest some old rearview mirrors set so they can see behind the outbuildings from in the house, like I have at my place. If anyone asks, it is because of bears. But it would help spot a person, also. I need to get a few more set up on my place, since I have been building and blocking my views.

Noah comes over and says Rose has invited us all to her place for dinner, this evening, if we can. I go back with Noah, Will and Shari follow in their vehicle.

Rose has made some bread using the quinoa she has been growing with some success. It adds a different flavor and texture, but is good. She used it in place of rice in the side dish and has made chicken fried steaks from some moose meat she had in her freezer. The salad is greens picked thinning her garden patch. A very good dinner, especially since I didn't have to cook it. We all talk about growing more of our own food out here and what all grows quite well. Rose used to work for a seed company in Fairbanks and did the research on new varieties at that time.

Dessert is a lemon cake, split and filled with lemon pudding and a cream cheese frosting on it. Oh, my. I love lemon almost as much as chocolate.

After dinner we are all almost too stuffed to move. Kara is the first one to go home and the rest of us just slowly follow along. I don't think I like days this interesting.

The next day, Will and Shari go in to get a dog and take the picture Rose has printed out for them to give the Troopers. That should help the case against Royal. The picture shows his face perfectly and also what he is trying to do.

Shari has her doctor's appointment and everything is going well. The doctor suggests she relax more. Well, with Royal in jail, maybe she can.

They find a lovely female mastiff at the pound. She is about 3 years old and quite well behaved and

trained.   Then they found 2 beautiful malamutes and
by the time they left, they had the start of a team.
The dogs had been brought in with harness, so they
were given the harnesses, also.   They find a deal on a
used sled and strap it on top the vehicle.   They are
going for the whole Alaskan experience.

Then they fill the rest of their vehicle and the sled
with dog food.   They pick up wire to make a dog run,
and soon have an overloaded vehicle.   The mastiff and
the malamutes check each other out, but seem inclined
to get along okay.

When they decided to get a dog, they were really
serious.   From none to 3 large dogs in one day was
quite a change.

They decided to put the dog run behind the house
and a bit to the side so the dogs could see anyone
coming up the drive.   When Roman and Thad pulled
up, Will was digging post holes.   He figured next trip,
he would buy some metal posts which would have been
simpler to place and last longer.   He thought he would
probably have to buy some concrete to keep the dogs
from digging out, but this should hold them, in the
meantime.   Roman says he is going in the next day and
can pick up posts since he is taking his trailer, and the
concrete, also, if Will would like.   So they figure out
what amounts of each will be needed and Shari asks
about a gate.   So a gate is added to the list.   Will
hands over a wad of cash.   Roman says to wait until
they get back, as they may not be able to find all that is
needed.

That night, Pal is nervous, pacing around in the
house until I finally check all the windows.   I don't see

anything, but hate to turn him out and maybe have a bear in the area or wolf that may hurt him. He thinks he is invincible, but I don't want him hurt. So I grab the 12 gauge with slugs and go out with him. He sniffs around the house and under each window. If it was a bear, it is the only one I ever saw that wanted to peek in windows.

As we come around the back corner of the house, 2 guys jump away from the wall and Pal immediately takes off after them. From the sounds, he is getting in his notice that they are not welcome. I call him back, when he reaches the edge of the yard. I don't want them to hurt him if they have a vehicle parked out of sight and maybe guns. He comes trotting back with a big doggy grin and shards of shirts hanging from his teeth. I think he may have gotten deeper than shirts from the screams once in a while.

I hear the motor start and it sounds like they are pulling in instead of leaving. I step to the side of the house and as they pull in, shooting from the windows of their SUV, I open fire with the 12 gauge and take out their front windshield and the back, also. The next shot is in the radiator and the third shot is just into the rig. They certainly found reverse in a hurry and back out a lot faster than they drove in. It looks like the SUV Royal was driving earlier. I guess his buddies are still looking for Shari.

Noah got back a short time after they left and mentioned seeing the SUV along the road, with steam coming from under the hood. I told him about the 2 guys and what I had done. He went over to let Will know then stopped to tell Kara and Rose and his Dad.

His Dad would notify the Troopers tomorrow in town.

I think I liked the good old days when it was only the bears I had to worry about.

Chapter 21

Rose planned on going to town the following Sabbath and asked if I would like to go with her. I had never thought much about religion or church, but thought it would be nice, so accepted.

She said she would be there by 7, as services started at 9:30 am. That would give us time to stop early during business only hours at the warehouse store and pick up some things before the crowd. That sounded good to me, also.

She said there was no actual dress code, just clean and covered although no one had ever said that, even. She usually wore either clean jeans and shirt or long skirt with pants under and shirt. She said she felt naked without pants covering her legs.

Sabbath morning, she was there, right at 7 am and we left right on time. She is not a slow driver so we made it to the warehouse store in good time for shopping before leaving for church. She picked up some cases of canning jars and some of the dehydrated or freeze dried storage food. There was some marked down burger and some skinless boneless chicken breast and she bought quite a bit of that. She has a cool chest in the pickup that plugs in to the lighter and keeps things cold. She also got some lunchmeat for the shack and some cigarettes that Kara sells. Then we headed for the little town south of Fairbanks, North Pole, where she goes to church.

I'm not sure what I expected, but this is a little church and everyone is very nice and friendly. It is like coming to visit family and we enjoy ourselves a lot. After services, there is a potluck and Rose has brought a large pan of rolls she had made and a dessert, another of those lemon cakes. Oh, yum.

We stop on the way home and pick up the ice cream Kara needs for the shack. The meat gets moved to cool bags with ice and the ice cream goes into the plug in cooler.

We stop and check the mail on the way home, at the little locked boxes in Fox.   It is only a 50 mile drive to check the mail.

Rose will be canning meat tomorrow, so asks if we should stop and invite Shari to join us, if I wanted to come, also.   This sounds good to me, I can always use some new ideas on meat canning.

So we stop and Shari is very happy to come over tomorrow.

Rose takes me on home, thanks me for going with her.   I can and do hope she will invite me again.   She says she seldom gets to go as the trip costs so much now.   Then she goes home to unload her purchases. This has been a very nice, pleasant day.

The next morning, I ride over with Noah.   He and his Dad and brother are finishing up the cabin, woodshed and the outhouse.   They have hauled some firewood for the woodshed and are cutting and stacking it whenever they have spare moments.   I hike on down to Rose's and Shari is already there.   They are cooking the meats in assorted ways.   They made some small meatloaves and are canning them in thin brown gravy.   The chicken, she roasted the night before and they are dicing it up. Some of the diced chicken gets covered in Buffalo Wing sauce and they use that to top pizza with.   Most of the rest, she cans in broth and uses in recipes calling for diced chicken.

They are browning a large pan of the burger to just can dry, to use in recipes, also.   A pint is the equivalent to a pound of browned burger.   Some, she added diced onion and celery and green bell pepper to, and will pour in a #10 can of diced tomatoes. That can be spiced any way when opened to use.

Shari is even taking notes. She really wants to learn how to do these things. She is also making a grocery list. I think Will is about to have a large hole in his bank account.

Roman and his sons have started buying barrels of gas and diesel each trip to town and storing them in the back of their woodshed. They also picked up a nice small generator in addition to the larger one he has in his shop trailer. He has been loading up on nails and screws, house wrap and vapor barrier rolls. He says he wants to build a large home someday and wants to buy it while it is available. So do his sons. He is buying roofing ever so often, also. He was thinking of building another shed like the woodshed to put building supplies in. He asked Rose if he could sell building supplies from here and also do diesel mechanic work. She told him yes, if he got insurance to cover it as she only had the policy listed at the driveway. He thought that over a bit and agreed, he would buy insurance. He offered to buy blanket coverage for the whole place as he said it wouldn't be any different in price. So she said yes. Her signs keep out the wussies, anyway.

The next few days, the guys put up another structure and roof it. Then start adding pallets of supplies in under it. They will pick up some T 1-11 next trip in and cover the walls so it is more secure. This may be the middle of nowhere, but there are still thieves.

That trailer is getting a good workout and is used every trip they make to town. They can haul a lot of material home on it and never fail to make the stop at the Transfer Stations. They have found enough windows to make a very nice greenhouse with real glass. Several metal clad insulated doors, assorted fixtures, electrical and bathroom. Kitchen cabinets and appliances. They are picky and only bring the very good condition items back. Now they are placing them with care in the new shed. It is going to require an addition very soon at this rate.

They have also been buying a lot of dry food supplies. One trip back, they also bring a dog. They said he followed them and they couldn't resist him. He turns out to be a pregnant female. So now they have a dog. They also build a run out the back door for the dog, so when they let it out, it has the pen right there handy. They decided Will had the right idea, so they also mix and pour concrete for the floor and around the posts to keep the pen easy to clean and no digging out. Until everything is set up and dry, they keep her tied to the bumper of one of the trucks or in the house with them. She seems to be well behaved and housebroken, so that is a plus. She is not a fancy looking dog, and looks more like what is known as an Alaskan sled dog and maybe something heavier built thrown in somewhere down the line. She has one blue eye and one brown eye from the sled dog line. She does not seem to bark, which is okay, but not much help for a watch dog. She does growl when something bothers her though. That night, they get to hear her howl and she does a very good job of it, too.

She settles in happily and adds one more creature to the collection in the area and soon to add more.

I want to build an earth bermed shelter as a barn, I think. That should help keep animals warm, if I manage to get goats. If I don't, it will be good storage. Maybe I should start it and try stocking it with supplies for animals, just in case I ever get some.

The next morning, I start laying out an area to build an earth bermed barn. I don't want it into the permafrost bank as that would defeat the purpose. So I guess maybe build on top the ground and haul dirt in around it. The area where nothing wants to grow very well should be a good spot. It is mostly rock. So I measure out and move a few rocks around, to give an idea how it will look. Then I move some more and think there are enough rocks here to make a foundation, of sorts. By the time my back is complaining loudly, I have a low foundation set out in the far corner of my yard. The larger flat stones I had scooted over into place, trying to have a fairly large one at each corner. I would have to come measure and square it later. I don't think it is all that square, but it is a barn after all. Square is over rated. So is level and straight.

At the lower end of my place is a large rock outcropping, so I take my pickup, a pick and grub hoe down to check it out. Maybe if there are enough rocks, I will try making a mostly rock barn, insulate the outside or inside, whichever, and dirt berm that to help make it warm for the animals. Should help it be fire proof or at least fire resistant. The more I think about it, the better I like it, so I start loading rocks into the pickup. I still have a couple bags of concrete in the shed, if they are not too hard, I will start using it to hold the rocks.

When I am unloading, Noah shows up and helps. He wants to help on building the barn, and offers to pick up more concrete in town, next trip. I tell him I don't have the money for it now, so it will have to wait. He just smiles and we keep on working. We haul several more loads of rocks up from the ledge down the hill. Most are rather flat and should be fairly easy to stack. Noah leaves after we get done with the rocks.

I have some long bolts I had picked up at the Transfer Station one time and brought home just in case. Well, this will be that case. I can set them in between the rocks and concreted in, then place through a board on top to nail to and hold the upper section of wall and roof on with.

Our piles of rocks are looking pretty good. I think we may have enough to make the lower 3 or 4 feet all rock and concrete, when I get some. That should deter a fire fairly well, if I put a metal roof on it.

I mix up the concrete I have on hand and start placing the rocks in the walls I have marked out. It doesn't go far, but it is a start.

I peel some more of the logs the guys brought as firewood. I think they will be part of the future barn.

Maybe I should cut 2 sides off and stack them, like kids toys. I should do that to the rest before peeling, will only have half the peeling to do then. So I get out the chainsaw and an old board to tack on the log and use as guide. I make a quick block for each end with a couple of 2x4's and nail 2 small pieces on each side to hold the log in place and start to work on that. If I have everything ready to go, once the rocks are stacked, it will be quick work to do the rest of the building. I am thinking of adding a short side walled upstairs for dry storage, also. Depends on how much material I have when it is being built.

Chapter 22

Noah, his Dad and brother drive in about the time I think I better quit on this job and take care of the other chores needing done. They have brought concrete, from the dog run they built and had left over. Well, maybe I am not so tired after all and the other chores will still be there.

With all of us working, it doesn't take long to have it looking like real walls.   It will still need more concrete, to continue, but it looks really good.   We placed rough cut lumber in slots in the walls to frame in 2 doors, then built the rocks up around them.   One 4 foot wide and the other 3 feet wide at the other end of the barn. We did not place then at the side closest to the driveway, so have to go to one end or the other to enter.   Seems like a good idea at the moment.

I run in and add dumplings on top the stew I have simmering on the stove.   I think it will feed us all.   I have some canned blueberries left from last year, so stick them on and add dumplings on top of them, too. Not a very well rounded meal, but it is filling.   I think as long as there is any type of dessert, the guys will like it.   Too bad there is no ice cream to put the hot berries and dumplings on.

The guys finish cleaning up the mess from mixing and working with concrete and come in for dinner.   I was right, they will eat anything with any type of bread on or in it.   The stew is new produce from the garden, not enough of any one thing to make a meal, but several small amounts of quite a variety.   I added a jar of cooked burger that had not sealed from the canning at Rose's.   A bit of powdered broth adds rich flavor and it is filling.

Will and Shari have been going to town and buying a lot of supplies.   Food, building and clothing, both for themselves and the new addition they are expecting. Shari wants to be set to stay out here without having to drive when the roads are bad in winter.   On one of their trips, they bring back a load of concrete and tell me Happy Birthday.   They had found a super sale on it, in town and could not resist.

My birthday is not for a few months yet and I try to refuse such a wonderful gift.   Shari gets a bit bent out of shape and says after all I have done for them, it is also a big thank you.

Wow, how can I refuse?   This is enough to do the barn and the floor in the ice house and chicken coop. Maybe even some for part of the floor in the barn. This is a lot of concrete.   They borrowed Roman's trailer and had it full and covered, just in case of rain. So far we have been lucky on our building projects with no actual heavy rain. Each of us have a sense of needing to get as much done as we can and stock up on all we can afford.   No one wants to talk about it, but the urgency is there.

Prices on food have been going up so fast, it shows, week to week on the shopping trips to town.   The shelves in a lot of the stores have been very thinly stocked and some have moved the shelf units farther apart to make it look like they have more supplies. Sometimes it is hard to find items normally considered staple goods.   Now it is buy it when you see it, it may not be available next trip in.   I really need to do more panning before the next trip to town.   Maybe I can buy the goat or two I have been wanting.   I better start cutting grass to dry for hay.   I have an old scythe and although it has been years since I used one, I guess I can get used to it again.   My main problem will be how to dry it.   I will have to cut along the roadway, as I don't have enough ground cleared and growing grass. The seed heads are forming on the native grasses, so I better start my cutting program in the next few days. It is a good thing the highway department is lax about mowing along the main roads.

I start early the next day, and soon find my rhythm. However, not too long after, I also find I have not done this in years and am going to be in pain in a large way, very soon. I better quit this for today. Maybe pound rocks or something easy.

I start working on the barn walls again. The walls are a good foot thick, maybe thicker. I'm not being too careful on making them totally even, it is still a barn. However, I am trying for fairly straight. I would rather the walls not fall down because I tilted them too much.

Rose shows up about the time I am totally worn out. She has brought me part of a roll of used roofing membrane to use as waterproofing against the sides of the building before dirt berming it. She has a lot of it, and is sharing it. We walk around the project and she comments on certain points. She suggests I make high narrow windows on first floor and use Plexiglas in them to keep it warmer and not so easy to break. That sounds like a good idea, I didn't want it dark in there, but also didn't want it easy to damage. We talk about how high the ceiling should be, on the ground floor. She says she usually goes for 7 feet at least. That way it doesn't feel so much like it is a cave and still low enough for holding heat in. She suggests I add a chimney just in case I ever have to heat it. If a goat is birthing, in cold weather, that may increase the chances of survival for the young one and mother, both. She also suggests I insulate the upper floor just in case I don't want to heat the upstairs storage, also. If I have enough insulation, I may do that. Hay doesn't need heated.

I need to find enough long poles, strong enough to span the distance to place in the walls to support the floor for upstairs. Down near the river are some stands of spruce that are needing thinned but are fairly straight and tall. I may just go liberate, ummm, borrow, some of those.

By evening, I am so tired and sore I feel like I have been run over by a truck or two. When Noah shows up, he hands me a weed whacker with a chain instead of string head on it. He said his Dad had it in the shop trailer and he thought it might be easier to cut hay with. Oh my, I think this is probably one of the nicer things anyone has ever done for me.

The next morning, I can barely move as I slide out of bed and creakingly stand up. I have aches where I didn't even know I had muscles. I slowly stretch and move and soon I have loosened up enough to get dressed and start the day. Okay, I guess the scythe is something to work into slowly.

After the morning chores, I take the weed whacker out and start along the roadway again. Oh yeah, this is a much better idea. It cuts the grass right at the ground and even small saplings. Goats won't mind the saplings, either. I check the grass I cut yesterday and it seems to be drying very well. I brought a rake along with me, and rake it into small windrows along the road to pick up later. I will have hay before I have a barn. But it has to be cut while the seed heads are full but not dropping yet or it is straw and worthless as animal food.   After raking, I go back to cutting, again.   I would like to have enough to fill the loft of the little barn.

The weed whacker is much easier on my back, arms and body in general.   I think I love that man.   Well, extreme like anyway.   He is so thoughtful, good worker, helpful and nice, just plain nice.   Well, he is pretty good to look at, also.   The fact that he is an excellent kisser is beside the point, we have been very careful not to repeat that.

I cut all along my driveway and down to the house, then go out and down to the wood lot, also.   I had nice wide sides on the roads, to act as partial firebreaks, so there was a lot of good thick grass along that.   This sure makes my place look good.   The main road is looking better, also.

I place some pallets side by side and make a raised area, near the barn but out of the way a bit.   Then I take the pickup out and gather the hay I had windrowed.   I placed it in one pile on the pallets. Then I gathered the first grass I had cut this morning. I spread it out better on the rest of the pallets to dry more.   I continue picking up the cut hay and spreading it on the pallets until I have quite a lot spread out and no more room to spread it.   It needed dried better so couldn't pile it.   I would have to go turn it every day until it was dry.

A lot of the stuff I cut along the main road had clover in it, in full bloom.   That would be excellent hay and I needed to keep it separate a bit from the plain grass hay.   Maybe I should pick up some clover seed in town and scatter it along my roads on the property.   It won't help this year, but should improve next year's hay crop.

After my day of haying, I am beat, yet again. Even using the weed whacker, I am sore and tired. I grab my chainsaw and go down near the river and cut enough long fairly straight poles to use as support for the loft floor in the barn. When I limbed them, I cut fairly close so there won't be much peeling to do on these. I'm glad spruce is so much lighter than Birch, small trees are easy to load and tie down on the pickup. They may drag once in a while, so I have to be careful. They aren't the only thing dragging.

By this time, most of the new woodsheds are fairly full. Having 2 years' supply of firewood on hand is wonderful. Every time I think of ever having to cut wood by hand, I cringe inside and vow to keep at least a full year ahead. What if my saw breaks, what if I can't afford gas, the possibilities are endless.

Chapter 23

The building projects on each property are all coming along very well. Rose would like another woodshed near her house, but can't enlarge her current one without closing her driveway or building a new driveway to the house. Finally she decides to just add it to the north side of her house and move the oil tank, since she doesn't heat with oil any more. She could put it right up next to the entry porch and use the 2nd door from the porch to carry wood in, without ever having to go completely outside. She says she is getting lazy in her old age.

Maybe we can do that after Will and Shari's is filled. They are close to having it done, now and so is Roman and his sons. Those guys have been working very hard on making the little cabin and outbuildings into a wonderful area. Rose and Kara wish they had met them when they first started building out here. Or before. Some of the "help" they have had has been less than stellar.

Roman has been stocking his building supply shed every time he goes to town. He has also been stocking the cabin with supplies they will need for winter. Will and Shari are doing the same and both groups ask us questions all the time about what they will need to make winter easier. When they found the fur dealer in town, they bought some excellent hats, mitts and mukluks for winter wear. They got some military surplus flight pants and parkas, then some bunny boots, which look like cartoon bunny feet. Big white air cushioned military surplus. I think they are the warmest boots ever made and feet sweat in them, very badly, but they don't freeze.

These guys have some money to spend so they can just go buy what they need. It would be easy to be jealous of that, but they are so nice and they share when we need something before we even realize what they are doing. They earned it, so no matter what, it is their right to use it as they want. I am super thrilled when Shari drives down the hill at their place in a little 6 wheeled ATV that looks like a small pickup. It has room for 2 people and a small dumpbed on the back for hauling dirt or whatever. That is the cutest little vehicle and she says it is very fuel efficient.

She has been dragging wood down to their house from the woods out back with it. Their dogs love running along beside her. I am glad she is never totally alone out there. She is starting to show her baby bump fairly well and says she is not sick at all now. Will cuts and hooks up the logs, she drags them down and unhooks, then back for the next load he has ready.

I ride up and back with her on her next trip, but don't want to slow them down as they have a good system going. So after one trip, I go over to see how Rose and Kara are doing. Kara has the shack open and I get an ice cream, then go on down the hill to see her Mom.

Rose is peeling posts to use as the uprights for her next woodshed. She has cleared out the area and leveled it some with the grub hoe. She said with the loose hydraulics on the backhoe, she would probably take out a wall of the house if she tried digging with it. She has hauled quite a bit of gravel to make the floor of the shed. She asked the guys to pick up any old rugs they find at the Transfer Stations for added floor in the woodsheds. Some that they have found are so nice, she is storing them in the shop. They will be fine in the small cabins she has been building for guests or family to have privacy if they visit. I like that idea and have used my old little cabin that way, too. I should put up a couple more and can use them for dry storage if needed. Maybe put them out through the woods on my place, not in my yard. That is what Rose is doing. A cabin here, a cabin there. Privacy and quiet for everyone.

When I get home, the pets are acting nervous and jumpy but soon settle down. I still get that feeling like someone is watching, once in a while and I guess it gets to the animals, also.

I decide to do laundry and go to get the sheets out of the little cabin. Someone has used it since the guys and did not make the bed as nicely as they did. Dang, I better start locking things again. Maybe the feeling of being watched was for real. Nothing seems to be missing, at least.

Pal sticks close to me while I do the laundry, I am glad of his company. Now I wonder what I did without a dog for so long. I know he would let me know before anyone came in the yard or got too close.

After hanging clothes and as the next load is washing, I go turn hay along my driveway and the small amount left out along the roadway. Some is ready to pick up, so I load it in the pickup.

I unload the hay after adding the rinse water, and turn the hay on the pallets. It is getting as dry as it needs to be, so I will have to hurry up on the barn.

After hanging the last load of clothes, I start on the barn walls again. I place heavy duty frames around future windows. Then back to the rocks and concrete. I am having a hard time going up a ladder with rocks or concrete so I guess it is time to switch over to log sections.   First, I place the bolts in concrete along the top of the wall, then drill holes in the plank I will use on top the rocks to nail the log sections to.   I place the planks before the concrete is set up, I may not have drilled the holes totally straight and want it to actually fit.   Probably not the right way, but it should work.   I have set bolts on up through the planks, also, to put through the log sections as I don't think nails will hold it very well.   It's a good thing I had a lot of those long bolts.

The guys show up after I have finished cleaning up the concrete mess.   They are a bit upset that I didn't wait for them to do the heavy stuff.   Well, they have stuff to do also and why should they feel obligated to come do my work?

This concrete seems to be the quickset stuff, so we go ahead and start stacking the logs I cut earlier.   We have to measure and drill, but it still goes quickly. Soon we have it high enough to set the poles across for the floor support for upstairs.   I will probably need some more pier blocks and add some uprights down the center of the building to support the weight of the upstairs floor if I start storing much up there, like feed and hay.   Well, hay anyway.   I mark where I would like an overhead haymow.   It will go directly over the widest door downstairs.   If I put in a pulley system and hooks, I can fill the loft with it.

 After the logs on the walls are notched out and the poles placed across, we continue stacking the logs up another 4 feet for the side walls.   If I had more logs, I would build the side walls higher, but I don't.   I will have to frame in the rest of the gable ends.   The guys want to know if I want a regular barn shaped roof on it. I am not sure how to make one of those. Roman says he does, and if I want, we can do it. However, we will have to build trusses for that. I am not sure I have materials for trusses, and have never used them. I am running low on salvaged materials with all these projects.

It is so late by now, my stomach is complaining loudly about the lack of food. Kara closed a while ago, so can't even go get a sandwich from her. I do have some pocket bread I made last night, so I can heat some chili and stuff those. So I invite the guys in and start opening chili and heating it. Then chopping some green onions from the garden and shred some cheese into a bowl. This will be a simple meal, but I hope it fills them up. I fix a large bowl of salad to go along with the chili and have some leftover chocolate fudge cake on the counter. Not the best meal I ever prepared, but not the worst, either. I set the salad on the table and the items to add to their sandwiches, then fill the pocket bread and place on plates and set around the table. Everyone is quick to sit and start in. I never have to worry about leftovers with this group.

Roman says we should build the floor upstairs then build the trusses on the floor to raise into place. Much easier than building them on the ground, then lifting up almost 2 stories into place. Makes sense to me. Noah places a gentle kiss on my lips as they go out the door, just a hint and a whisper of a kiss.

In the morning, I am up and hauling all the 2x6's I can find over to the barn. Maybe I have enough to do the floor. I also need to place the future staircase.

Too bad I don't have one of the pull down staircases, although they might be hard to use carrying a load. I think I will leave open spaces to fork hay down into hay racks for feeding. Maybe make a small raised edge around each one so I don't just walk off into open air some winter day while feeding. So, I need to place where things are going to go, downstairs before trying to do much upstairs.

I think I will put a small room in the center to store dry feed in, easier than hauling large bags upstairs and then back down to feed. That will help support the upstairs, also. I add a chimney so I can heat the barn if needed. Not sure where to put a chimney with hay in the upstairs. Maybe an insulated pipe out through the downstairs wall and then up at the gable end of the building. It won't have as good a draft, but it should still work. I will have to put a cleanout at the bottom of the elbow so I can brush the pipe often, since it will be outdoors. Now to check all the stovepipe I have stored. I think I have an insulated elbow. I can strap the pipe to the building all the way up, to support it, if I use a metal pipe to strap it to, then strap that to the building.

While I am sorting through pipe, the hair on the back of my neck feels like it is rising. I whirl around and see someone duck in behind some trees, farther out in the forest. Dang, what a time to forget to bring Pal with me. I know better.

I pretend not to know the man is there and slide my handgun into my hand and start walking back up the hill to the house. After I get to the upper edge of the trees, I fire a couple of shots into a stump, just as warning. I don't know who this is, and it could be one of the guys from Shari's home town or just some fool looking for access to the land below mine. Either way, I am not happy about it.

When I get to the house, I let Pal out and keep him near me. I worry that someone may hurt him if he catches them on my property. I'm not too worried about them, they take their chances if they are trespassing.

As the days progress, we finish up my barn, and I put the now dry hay up in the loft. I cut more as I find it and started putting the pallets in the barn and drying the grass in there. We are going into August and it is usually our rainy season. We have been lucky to have a dry summer so far and no local fires to worry about. Rose's new woodshed is finished and starting to be filled. I have panned a small amount of gold out and sold it. It was enough to buy some much needed supplies and 2 young goats. I was lucky enough to find 2 that are unrelated, a male and a female. Now I will have to build some fences as goat proof as possible. Especially around my garden. I also bought as many seed packets from a local nursery of Alaskan type seeds. Most are heirloom, so if possible, maybe I can save seeds from them. Carefully, I pack them in a canning jar with a good lid and store it out in the ice house. I also store several boxes of ammo out in the ice house in canning jars with good lids. These are placed in an old tote that fits in behind the shelf unit I built in the back. I placed an old handgun in the tote, wrapped in an oily rag and then in a zippered plastic bag. The inner and outer doors are always locked on this building, so I consider them quite secure. Later, I add a shotgun and shells for it, also. Since I seem to have folks hanging around in the woods, I cover everything I carry to the ice house, so no one can see what is being stored. I'm starting to feel a bit paranoid.

Chapter 24

Shari comes by the next day and looks worried. I think this is the first time I have ever seen her out driving by herself.

She says she and Will have found signs that someone has been camping around the back of their property, where they can watch the house. She is worried that it is the fellows from her hometown. I agree it probably could be, but really don't want to scare her more than she is already.

I ask if she has heard anything about Royal and what is happening with that.

She says somehow, the Court didn't see how he was a danger and let him loose. They suggested he head home, but no plane tickets saying he did. The Trooper is upset and so are Will and Shari. Uh-oh, this does not sound good.

She says he only stayed in office as Sheriff through intimidation and voter fraud. So many had signed the voting lists that have been dead for almost 100 years that it was fairly obvious.

While we are standing in the yard, talking, we suddenly lost balance and just as suddenly, regained it. Oops, a small trembler. This was Shari's first and she did not like it. I reassured her they were usually harmless and happened quite often up here. She turned on the radio in her SUV and finally found a station we could hear through the static. Seemed to be quite a few earthquakes happening around the world, but none were major. Some damage and some loss of property. Nothing too bad, but we both felt a sense of something not quite right.

She decided to get home and check on Will, I went to check on the canned goods on my shelves. Right then and there, I decided to add better bars across each shelf to keep jars on them. Nothing had fell, but some had jiggled to the edge. I found some 1x2s left from roofing and started fastening them along the shelves, a couple of inches above the shelf. That should help a lot. After finishing mine, I go over to see if Rose and Kara need any help fixing theirs. Rose has very low ones on hers and would like higher ones on them and Kara has none. So we find more 1x2's and start with the screw gun and fasten them up, starting on the top shelves first. Nothing like a small wake up trembler to remind us we live in earthquake country. Rose has not had a problem with hers even through the 7.9 that shook the State several years ago, but would just rather not take a chance on one larger or closer.

After I get home, I feed my animals and make sure they have water. The chickens are big enough now to be considered chickens, not chicks. I would like to have got a few more as these seem to be about half males. Noah built a small chicken ark that rolls along between rows in the garden and lets the chickens fertilize and feed on weeds at the same time. An unlucky vole wandered into reach one day and they had meat with their greens. 3 of the roosters are very friendly and good natured, so I put them in a separate pen. I think as a gift, I will give one rooster and one hen to Rose and to Shari, so they can start their own fresh egg factories. Since these are nice, we will each have one and save them from the ax. The hens are all very good natured, which is one reason I got these 2 breeds. Large, good natured and pretty good layers and brooders, also. The other males will be nice chicken dinners as soon as I find someone that don't mind chopping off their heads. I may have them all winter, everyone has made pets of them.

I make another trip to town with the little bit of gold I have panned in the last couple of days. I buy feed for the chickens and the goats. I stock up on salt blocks and mineral blocks. I find some building supplies at the Transfer Station and finish loading my pickup. There are a couple of very nice rugs also, that go over the whole load, then my tarp and net and I am headed for home again.

Just after I cross the last large bridge, my pickup has some steering problems and I almost go off the road. I slow way down and proceed with extreme caution. As I proceed, I see that several trees are down along the road that I had not noticed before. These are close enough to come get for firewood. I turn my radio on, just to see if maybe that was another earthquake. All I find is static and dead air. That is not unusual with my radio and I think nothing of it until I get closer to home and as I start past Will and Shari's, I see them outside, sitting on the ground, holding each other. Something is wrong so I pull in.

Shari is crying and Will is upset. This does not look good. "Is it the baby?" I ask as I stop.

"No, Bubble Bump is fine. But I think the rest of the world is in trouble." she replies.

"The early reports are of massive damage and loss of life all over the world," Will says.

They have been using a broadband radio he bought a while back and are monitoring the short wave stations. None of the usual stations are on the air. He says the reports out of the Anchorage bowl area say there is no more Anchorage, no more Seattle, no more cities left standing around the world. Major fires from ruptured pipelines. The underground facilities everyone thought were foolproof and completely safe have either collapsed or flooded out. Whole countries are no more. Islands have disappeared and a few new ones have emerged only they used to be inland mountains. There is speculation that possibly 2 or more of the countries developing nuclear weapons may have detonated at various places at about the same time and set off worldwide earthquakes of a magnitude beyond the Richter Scale.

We go inside their house and find only a few items out of place and it seems sound. I want to stop and check on Kara and Rose on my way home to see what damage my place may have sustained.

I pull into their driveway and see that Roman's cabin and buildings seem to be okay. I go on down the hill and the guest cabins seem to all still be standing. Kara's house looks okay from outside. I stop and go to the door. No one answers so I go on down to her Mom's. Kara is there and we go inside. Rose is fine and picking up a few items that had fallen. Nothing major seems to have happened and the house looks okay. Kara says her place is fine, also. I tell them about thinking my pickup is breaking down. We laugh but it is not much of a laugh.

If Fairbanks didn't get hit very hard, soon there are going to be thousands of hungry people looking for food wherever and however they can find it. I tell them what I heard at Will and Shari's. There was no mention of damage to the Interior city or towns. We are far out of town, but not that far if they still have fuel to drive. All the military bases are a worry, also. That is a lot of people needing food in the immediate area.

Since it is late August, the nights are starting to get fairly dark again for a few hours. None of this is good news. I tell them I planned on giving Rose the 2 chickens to start her own small flock with, but now she won't be able to buy food for them. It may be too late to harvest grass seed, also. It is a good thing that chickens will eat just about anything. She says she will feed them whatever she is eating. Just like her dog and cats will have to do.

I have to get home and see what damage I have and how my animals are doing. As I pull into my yard, I see a stranger sitting on my steps waiting for me. When he sees me, he places his hands on top his head in a classic prisoner pose. He holds this as I walk toward him with my handgun in my hand. "Who are you and why are you here?" I ask.

"My name is Jeremy Rhodes and I killed Rod and Rob before they could hurt Shari. I caught your goats after the quake and put them back in the pens. I've been keeping an eye on Will and Shari's place since Royal and his buddies showed up. I don't want to hurt any of you but I really, really need a meal and someplace to stay, if possible. I know you should just turn me in, but honestly, I won't hurt anyone here."

Strangely enough, I believed him. It had to be someone they knew, to get so close to each guy and knife them while they waited in ambush for Will and Shari. I asked him exactly what happened that day, then said "Wait, why don't we go over and let you tell it to everyone here and we will decide what to do. After I check in the house first to see if everything is okay?

He said he checked under the house and it looked

solid and all right. So I unlocked the door and he went in ahead of me. There were some pictures off the walls and a few items fell from shelves in the living room, but overall, it looked pretty good.

We stopped at Rose's and she and the guys and Kara followed us over to Will and Shari's. Shari was shaken to see Jeremy but hugged him saying she knew he wouldn't hurt her. Seems he is her cousin.

Once we were all introduced, we waited for the story.

Jeremy started right from when they left the airport. He only came along to be the calm voice of reason, he thought, so they could talk over some legal matters needing cleared up by the death of Shari's folks. They did not think Rod was all that bad, and left him some property jointly with Shari, in their Wills with Rights of Survivorship. Rod decided he wanted it all. But Jeremy didn't know that until he was tied in the back of the SUV and heard what they were planning. He was to take the blame and they were going to use her own rifle to shoot her and if they had a chance, Will, also. Rob was only backup and to make sure Will didn't show up too soon after Rod had his little talk with Shari. Jeremy finally managed to work loose from his bonds while they trashed the house. He went in as they were going out the back and they did not see him. He found the large sharp knife where they stuck it into a sofa back. He followed Rob first and came in behind him as he hid behind the old outhouse. He was making too much noise to hear Jeremy who had been in Special Forces in the military, slip up behind him and slit his throat without a sound. He quickly stuffed him into the outhouse and then stalked Rod. He found Rod just as he was taking aim at Will. He wanted to taunt and punish Shari, so he was going to shoot Will right in front of her. The other woman (me) being there didn't even slow down his plans. He figured he would get to punish 2 women instead of just one. Jeremy slid silently up behind him and stuck the knife up under his ribs just as he started to squeeze the trigger and the rifle went off. There wasn't time to hide him or the rifle as we started directly for the sound of the shot. Jeremy just had time to get himself hidden before we got to the body. Then, the Trooper showing up, really made it impossible to do anything and Jeremy was afraid they would haul him in and he would never see the light of day again. He had been keeping an eye on Royals' buddies since they were now wandering the woods out here, also. He apologized for stealing food once in a while, but eating berries and roots and small rodents just was not a good diet. He was sorry he took my cinnamon rolls in the greenhouse, but just could not resist. When was I going to make some more?

Well, since the earthquake, we had no idea whether or not there were any Troopers left to come out or if there were any type of Court system left in the State. We talked it over while Jeremy sat in the other room, and decided he probably had saved several lives by the 2 he had taken. If Will and Shari were willing to have him stay here, the rest of us had no problem with that. They were willing. He was very surprised when we told him the decision.

Then talk turned to the earthquakes and Will turned

the shortwave radio back on for us to hear the updates. There were still a few HAM operators on the air and trying to let everyone know the extent of the damages. It sounded like the earth as we knew it was totally gone. There may still be a few small towns and villages here and there, but the roads, trains and shipping was gone. All the major cities, also gone. It was hard to think that Fairbanks may be the largest city left on earth. It had no means of supporting itself, so it soon would cease to exist as a city, either.

I finally got home and unloaded my pickup. It would probably be the last load of anything I would ever be able to buy in town, ever. This was it, there won't be any more. Noah helped me put the feed away and unloaded the building supplies and rugs into the barn.

We are both silent as we part and he goes back to his camper which weathered the quake fairly well.

The next morning, we awaken to a freak snowstorm. There is about a foot of heavy wet snow on everything and more coming down. Oh, this isn't good for the survivors in town. If they have no electricity most won't have heat. As deep and heavy as the snow is, no one will be driving out this way, anyway, so maybe it is good news for us.

I go out and make sure my animals are all closed up in their pens and buildings. I drain my water tank and tip the washing machine to drain the pump. I start filling all the water containers from the spring and storing them in the old ice house and in the house. The new ice house is also loaded up with some half full containers of water to allow to freeze, later, for ice.

The snow continues all day and there is the crashing of tree limbs breaking from the load on limbs still covered in green and gold leaves. Trees are bending and the brush is almost flat on the snow banks. The wind has come up, so it is blowing drifts across the roadway.

I ask Noah if he wants to try making it over to be with his Dad and brother. He says no, he is comfortable where he is, but if it gets much colder, could he move into the little cabin out back? It does have a small wood stove in it. Well, yes, it would be nice to have him here.

The snow keeps falling and during the night, the temperature starts dropping. I feel sorry for anyone out in this weather and the poor folks without homes now are to be prayed for.

Early the next morning, I hear the sound of a snow machine coming in my driveway. It is the fellow we delivered firewood to, this summer. He comes to the door and says he is just checking to see if I am okay and is going over to check on Rose, Kara and the new folks. He asks about the earthquake so we tell him what we have heard on the radio at Will and Shari's. He is dumbfounded and just shakes his head. I ask him if he will be okay and he says yeah, he has over a year's supply of gas for his snow machine and chainsaw and seldom ever went to town, anyway. I send him on his way with a bag of cinnamon rolls to either keep or share at each stop he is making this morning and invite him back for a meal on his way home. He accepts after thinking it over a second or two.

After he leaves, Noah comes to the door and I let

him in. He has shoveled a path from the house to the barn and to the woodshed. I fix breakfast and he is very happy to come in and get warmed up and a hot meal. After breakfast, I start bread dough and a large pot of stew from the remnants of the garden.

Chapter 25

I am so glad I have kept the garden harvested all summer as things ripened. Just a couple of days ago, I transplanted some lettuce I started late, kale and mint. It was now protected on my sun porch. I set it up with some LED grow lights I was checking out that a friend had sent me. My little solar panels were also on the porch in the windows and charging the batteries on any clear day.

I gear up and go out to care for the goats.   They are
enjoying the snow, at the present.   I think after a while
they may get tired of it just like most humans do.   At
present, I am thinking it may be saving us from some
unpleasant encounters with town folks.   Maybe by the
time they decide to head this way, they won't have fuel
for the trip.   Right now, the only way they could reach
us is by snow machine and they would have to be
hauling extra gas for the trip.

Late afternoon, the guy on the snow machine stops
back by to let us know the latest news from the other
direction.   He found everyone warm and cozy and at
Kara and Rose's they were even happier.   Their family
in town had rounded up some motorcycles and trailers
right after the earthquake, loaded up all they could find
and came home.   They got to the place just before the
snow hit too hard.   They said the bridge was out just
north of town and they came through the river.   The
next bridge was cracked and they went over it one at a
time, being very careful, the lightest loads first.   Then
at the last large bridge, they again crossed in the river as
the bridge looked like it was not safe.   Town had been
hit harder than the reports stated.   The underground
utility tunnels under the Bases and under downtown
Fairbanks had all collapsed and no utilities were
working.   The runways were all buckled and broken.
No flights could enter or leave, except helicopters and
only if they had enough fuel in the tanks as the tank
farm was on fire.   The roads going south from
Fairbanks were clogged with traffic thinking they could
drive somewhere and get away from the disaster.   No
one was headed north but them.

Both of Rose's great-grandchildren made it out with their parent. Their community had increased, but Rose and Kara both planned on them being there in emergencies, anyway. Some of the little extra cabins were just for each adult to have their own place. The "adopted" ones were also welcome and also had been planned for. They hadn't exactly planned on the one grandson bringing both of his girlfriends out, though. That could get interesting in the days ahead.

We shared our meal with the man and he accepted another bag of rolls and some bread to take on his ride home. He left soon after and we were glad he had stopped by. That was the best load of firewood we ever delivered.

Noah and I sat and tried to figure out exactly what was going to happen next and how to deal with it. We know we could survive out here, if we are left alone. It sounds like Wasilla may now be ocean front property. So the coastline has changed drastically. I am wondering how Interior is going to change if the ocean levels are rising or have risen. Most of the Yukon and Tanana valleys are not very much above sea level. What if we now could catch ocean fish just down in our valley? We will probably have to wait until the coming summer to find out about that.

The next morning, I awaken to the sound of the goats in a panic and loud barking from Pal. I jump out of bed, grab a gun and head for a window toward the barn. I look out and see a very large grizzly trying to tear into the barn. I am so glad it has rock lower walls. I open the window and sight carefully. I gently squeeze the trigger and the bear slumps down. He starts to rise, then slumps over again. I will wait a bit before going to check. Noah comes racing around the corner of the house pulling on his coat and hat. I unlock the front door and he comes on in.

"What on earth…?" he starts. I just say "Grizzly."

After a few minutes, we put on some wet weather boots and heavy mitts and coats and go check to see if it is really dead. As we wade through the snow, Noah asks if this is a usual occurrence. "No, actually I have never shot a grizzly before," I answer.

We walk up on the bear from behind with guns at the ready. If the bear even twitched, it was going to get shot a whole lot more. It didn't twitch. I poked its eye with the rifle barrel, no response. I think it is dead.

We drag the bear over away from the barn a ways, and spread it on its back with legs out. I pull out a quick change utility knife to start skinning. Noah asks why I use that. I tell him they stay sharp, only have to twist the handle to change blades if they get dull and they work very well.

I make the first cuts to make a nice shaped hide when finished and then start skinning. Noah starts on the other side and it does not take us long to skin the bear. It is an adult male in very good condition. There are no bad odors, only the usual butchering odors, so it must have fattened up on blueberries. I will cure and smoke the hams and maybe try making bacon if there is enough meat over the ribs. I bring out some large clean totes and we start trimming fat off the body to render for lard. I cut down through the fat over the ribs to the ribs and find it is over 2 inches thick. I will try making it into bacon. I cut both sides off, peeling it down to the ribs. And place it in the tote with the picnic shoulders, hocks and hams to be cured. The ribs and back and brisket will be used as roasts, BBQ ribs and maybe corn the brisket.

We soon have the bear cut into nice cuts of meat and take the totes to the sun porch to keep them cooler than in the main house. The hide will be worked on in the evenings. I did skin the head and feet out before they were cut from the body. That is easier to do at that time. But I will still have to flesh it out better and salt the hide. I cut the head from the body and consider trying brain tanning the hide. The neck has a lot of meat on it so maybe make mincemeat from that. I sort through the gut pile and remove the heavy fat deposits through it all and around the kidneys. This adds a lot more fat to the pile to render for lard.

After the bear is butchered up. The gut pile is dragged over as far as we could get it from the house, with all the snow. We took care of the goats and let Pal know what a good dog he was for barking at the bear. He showed no interest in going after the bear, so he is a smart dog.

When we get back in the house, I check the meat and it is cooling nicely. I mix up the cure to put on the meat and start by putting a layer in a tote, then a layer of meat, and another layer of cure. The heavy hams go on the bottom and the thin bacon slabs go on top all covered in a thick layer of dry cure. The first totes used are rinsed out and set to dry. I put a towel over the meat in the other tote so nothing gets into it. The extra cure mix is left beside it to be added the next day when the meat is turned and checked. The hams are very nice shaped and should be good.

While I was doing that, Noah filled my woodbox and started breakfast. We worked together all through the day, clearing snow off roofs where we could and shoveling trails around the yard. I finished harvesting the greenhouse and the garden. The large tomato plants I brought in last week, are doing fine on the sun porch. It isn't warm enough for them to grow, but all the green tomatoes on them would slowly ripen and we would still have fresh tomatoes into at least January. The late zucchini would be great fried and as soup or as bread. I placed them out on a shelf on the sun porch, also. It is more of a walk-in fridge in winter than a sun porch, but it is nice to have the fresh veggies most of the winter.

The extra fat we had cut off the bear, I coarse ground and set on the back of the wood heater to slowly render into lard. It would be a welcome addition to the food stores and make excellent pastries and doughnuts.

I only had a small fire going in the wood stove, to keep the chill off the house, so didn't have to worry about the lard burning as it rendered. I set the leftover stew pot on the stove to reheat while we worked, also. When we came in at lunchtime, it sure was nice to have it ready and the water hot for a drink. I keep a large pot of water on the wood stove all the time for wash water and to do dishes or bathe. When I am working outdoors, I also put the teakettle on the wood stove to have it ready for a hot drink. Noah was used to having running water and electricity, so this was going to be a learning experience for him. The good thing is, he seems willing to learn and go along with it.

The rest of the day, we work at making sure everything is as ready for winter as we can make it. In some ways, I hope this doesn't last and that we get our usual Indian Summer but knowing the possibility of hungry people heading out from town if the roads clear, makes me selfishly wish this was the actual start of winter. There is nothing I can do to help all the thousands in town. I can help the folks in my immediate area.

The next day, we build in the room and hay ricks in the barn. All I can hope is that I cut enough hay to last the winter, for the goats. I have never raised goats so am not sure how long it takes to gestate or how long until the young are weaned. I don't know how much to feed them a day, even. I better start reading my books and see if I have the information there. This will be a learning experience that I will have to learn and fast, no room for mistakes.

It starts snowing again, late in the afternoon and continues into the evening. Maybe winter has set in early.

We settle into a routine, of shoveling snow, packing firewood and caring for the animals. The meat is curing nicely and soon we have to go find some alder bushes for wood to smoke the meat. I hope it isn't too cold to take a smoke well. The bacon sides are cured first, so I hang them to dry. The lard rendered out very well and I use the leftover cracklings as flavoring in a batch of cornbread. I heat the lard to boiling and pour it into hot jars and seal. After they are cold, I will store them in the pantry in a cool dark area. After the hams are smoked, I will try sharing with Rose and Kara and also with Will and Shari. Best if we all keep helping out, I am thinking.

The hams are finally cured and I have found a nice stand of Alder brush near the roadway to cut and peel for the smoke. Noah and I finally have enough peeled that it should do the whole batch. I sewed some cheesecloth bags to hold the hams in and we will place the bacon sides flat on screen, so they hold their shapes. It seems to be warm enough during the day to smoke and I bring them to the sun porch at night. It only takes a few days to have them with enough smoke to consider done.

We decide to try our hand at snowshoeing over to see Rose and Kara. By the time we are about halfway there, we realize neither of us are in shape for this. So we turn around and go home. At the rate we are going, it would have taken us all day just to go a couple of miles. If this were a needed trip, yes, but not just to visit and share some hams.

Will and Shari show up a couple of days later. They have a plow on the front of their little 6 wheel ATV and have made a small road to each property. They said they realize gas is a premium item now, but if we can keep some sort of trail open it will be better for us all. Will shares the latest news from his radio. None of it is good.

The entire world has been affected by the quakes and no cities are left standing, anywhere. Ones along oceans have slid into the seas, civilization has just stepped back in time a few hundred years and not a lot of the current population have any idea how to live in those times. The only hope is that there are people with the knowledge to make and operate old fashioned tools and equipment. Even a lot of the Amish folk now hire or rent modern tools and equipment, just as long as they don't do it themselves. So not even as much knowledge with them on old farming practices.

Much of Southeast Alaska is apparently bare hillsides since the giant tsunamis washed through. Most of the Pacific Northwest is the same. The aftershocks are so bad in some areas that what buildings did survive are unsafe to go into. More people have died from cave-ins in apartment buildings and underground facilities. The huge volcano expected to erupt somewhere near Yellowstone seems to have dissipated by flowing into large unknown faults running along the east side of the Rockies and passing through near the former site of Denver. All the government underground facilities there are now full of lava. Washington DC is under water, so is New York City as far as anyone can tell. Florida is a few small islands. The new inland sea that used to be the Misssissippi Valley now has dolphins and whales. South America and North America no longer join. Europe, Asia and Africa are the same, now separate continents, separated by oceans. No one has heard from Australia or New Zealand.

The early snows of the Alaskan Interior have reached far down into Canada. People that survived the earthquakes are succumbing to the cold. The fear of outbreak of diseases has escalated because of the inability to bury the dead. Rodents, the usual carriers of disease, run rampant in the ruins. Looters are being shot on sight. So far, there does not appear to be any organized raiding.

After all this unhopeful news, we visit a bit and Shari is nervous now about the birth of her child soon. I offer to help but tell her to ask Rose as she is closer. I will be happy to help, though. She thinks she has enough clothes for the baby and did buy a lot of disposable diapers for the first few months and then will switch when she runs out to the cloth ones she already purchased. I will make a small Arctic hare fur bunting for the baby.

When they leave, they take their ham and one each for Kara and Rose. I divide the bacon up and share it for each household, also. I smoked the hocks, so they would be good seasoning for beans and shared those, also. I don't volunteer what type of meat it is, and they didn't ask.

The bacon is a little different but acceptable when we try it for breakfast the next day. I will have to practice cutting it thinner.

As we are eating breakfast, Pal starts growling at the door. We look at each other and head to the window to see what is out there. I see a large black bear out in the trees heading to the gut pile and Noah sees 2 guys, also sneaking through the trees, unaware of the gut pile or conflict of interest about to happen. The guys are only watching the house and have guns drawn and pointing toward us. This is something I consider offensive, so I grab the rifle leaning against the wall near the window. As I start to open the window, the bear decides these hairless bipeds are after his meal and steps in.   He takes a swipe at one and practically takes his head off, at the sound, the other one turns and pulls the trigger at the same time.   His 1st round goes high and wide and then he fires again, directly into the bear's belly.   The bear already thinks the guy is a thief, now he is enraged with a belly ache, too.   The bear takes another swipe with his paw and tears out the man's throat.   Then I shoot the bear.   Even though he has saved us a lot of problems in the future, I really don't want him as a neighbor and once a bear finds food anywhere, they always come back checking just in case there may be more.   At this rate, we are only going to have my least favorite meat for the winter.   But I can't pass up free meat, so we once again spend part of the day skinning and butchering.   There is nothing to be done for the 2 men and I recognize them as the 2 that came out with Royal to harass Shari.   I'm pretty sure with all this snow before freeze-up, that we can still dig graves for them.

We drag them and as many parts as we can find up out of the woods and straighten them out so they don't stiffen in bad positions.   I don't want them in my yard, so we walk out to the roadway.   There is a small gully over on one side of the road, with a nice dirt bank above it and we decide to just cover them there.   I really do not feel too sorry that they are gone.   I just wish I knew what happened to their leader.   I would have preferred the bear took care of him.

We drag the men out to the gully, push them in and start knocking the bank down over them.   We try to at least make it deep enough with dirt and a lot of rocks, to deter scavengers from digging them out.   It should freeze solid soon and that will help over the winter, anyway.

In the snow, the yard now looks like a bloodbath has taken place here. The grizzly at least had a bit more snow after we finished with him. It is cloudy, so I will pray for snow tonight to cover this mess up also.

I think we enjoy the bear meat more after it is cured and smoked, so I start this curing again. This was a large very fat old male, so he has enough fat over his ribs to again make some bacon. It is very fatty bacon, but will be all we will ever see again, unless someone out here has hogs. I have not heard of any, that does not mean there aren't. I doubt if any of the folks on up the road know I have chickens and goats.

As long as the weather stays near freezing but not too cold, I can still smoke the hams and bacon after they cure.

Chapter 26

We decide the old gut pile and now the new one is too much to leave laying in the edge of the yard for more bears to come around for. They don't hibernate until later in the winter and are always looking for more food to keep their weight up. We break the old pile loose from the snow onto a tarp and pull the new pile on, with it. The two of us drag the tarp out along the roadway as far as we can make it, on past the graves of the men. At least it won't be so close to the house and my animals. I go back and bring out a few small traps and a few large snares. It is not trapping season yet and pelts won't be prime, but we may not have the chance for getting furs later in the winter or as easily. I set the small traps on obvious small game trails close but not too close to the bait. I do not want to catch the ravens and jays that will come feed. I go farther out and make some snare sets even farther out on possible trails toward the bait. Then I place sticks to make open areas less desirable for predators to walk on to get to the bait, leaving my snared trails as the best routes. I don't think we will have a game warden showing up to cite me for trapping out of season.

Noah wants to learn about skinning and preparing hides, so we work on the grizzly and the black bear hides all evening. Since the grizzly has been salted a while, it is easier to work on, fleshing it nicely down. We comment on how human the hands and feet look, skinned out and decide to help the antisocial signs around the place by tacking the skinned parts to the signs. It will give the jays something to pick at during lean times ahead. Early the next morning, we go check my traps. We have a marten and a fox close to the pile, the snares are still empty. We take them home after I reset the traps. The fur looks better than I thought it would, so I am careful on the skinning and stretching them to tan and use for clothing, later. They dry very fast, so I cut the skulls open and smear the brains over the flesh side of the hides and work it in to help soften the hides.

Late afternoon, we check the traps and snares again, but nothing during the day.

The following morning, we find 2 wolves in the snares and those will add a good fur supply for garments, later. I carefully remove any sign they were caught and reset the snares, also. It looks as though they were alone, so no other wolves saw them caught.

We take them home and skin them out, that evening. I save the skulls to open later for the brains as these hides will take longer to dry. Once they are dry, I lightly sand the surface before adding the brains. This removes the membrane that makes it hard to tan a hide at home.

We continue checking the traps twice a day and manage to catch a couple more marten and another fox, then I pull the traps and only leave the snares. I don't want to kill all the animals in the area. I will trap farther out and in other directions later in the winter when fur is more prime. These are all in very good shape though, so they are getting prime very early this year from the weather.

The hams and bacon are done and we sample to see how it is. I like this one a bit better for bacon, the hams are about the same. Maybe I am just getting more practice and better at making it.

The fellow with the snow machine comes over to check on us and brings 2 caribou on his sled. He said he was out setting up his trap line when he came across the small herd from the White Mountains near here. He shot 3 young bulls as that would not harm the small herd any. He kept one and was bringing one for us and one for the others to share. I gave him a large ham and a side of bacon since he did not get any of the last one. He was surprised that I cured and smoked meats. I told him I would make sausage from some of the caribou if he wanted to come back in a few days for some. It would take about 2 weeks. He offered to go back for part of his caribou to use also, for a larger share. I told him if he had brown sugar and black pepper I would make all he wanted as I had plenty of salt and could share the salt.

We started skinning and by the time we were done skinning, he was back with most of his caribou. He helped finish cutting them up and then we cleaned out some of the intestine to make sausage casings out of. We squeezed then clean then poured water down them. We soaked them in salt water and then rinsed yet again, turning them inside out. The next soak was even stronger salt water to leave then in until ready to use.

We cut out the backstraps for steaks, and made some nice roasts from parts of the hams. The rest was mostly cut to grind up for sausage and burger.

I have a large, heavy duty meat grinder and with 2 guys helping, we deboned and ground a lot of meat that afternoon. The man's name was Al and he was delighted to learn how to make sausage. I let him look through my notes and cookbook and he picked out a couple of sausages he really liked. The Swedish Sausage sounded good to us all, and we had plenty of potatoes and onions to try it with, so we decided on that one. Then a basic recipe with only black pepper as seasonings besides some brown sugar and salt. It is nice in a lot of recipes. Then we decide to make some pepperoni, also. Pizza sounds very good.

We divide up the meat and weigh it out into piles required for the recipes. We tripled most of the recipes to make sure everyone had some of the finished product. The rest we packaged as plain burger to divvy up for each household.

While I packaged, the guys peel potatoes and onions for the Swedish Sausage. We have the counters and table divided up for each flavor sausage and we each start making. Then we rinse the casings yet again and turn them right side out. We stuff the mildest sausage first. The end of the casing is tied twice, very firmly into 2 knots. If one gives way, the other should hold. Ever so many inches we twist the sausage roll to make links. Only so much casing will push onto the tube from the grinder at one time, so we make several loops of each flavor sausage. We try to make each flavor into different length sausages. They do have slightly and not so slight difference in colors, but better safe than sorry.

I build up a bigger fire in the smokehouse and we hang the finished sausage loops from racks I have hanging in there. The double knots at the ends have to be carefully handled so nothing comes undone. Once they start drying, they will stay tied much better.

It is getting a bit late, so I fix us some dinner and Al joins us. Chicken fried caribou steaks with cream gravy and mashed potatoes, fresh salad and rolls. Al pats his tummy after dinner and laughs, saying he has ate better and talked more today, than he has in years. I offer him the little cabin for the night, if he don't have to get home and he can take some of the meat over to Rose, Kara, Will and Shari, tomorrow, if he likes. Noah is still using his camper so the cabin is empty. He decides that would be nice, so goes on over and starts a fire in the heater in the cabin. He comes back and we all visit a while. Then I check the smokehouse one last time for the night and add wood. The weather is a little warmer, so I am trying to speed the smoking up by running it night and day. The black bear is done so I will send some over with Al tomorrow for the rest.

I fix breakfast the next morning and Al offers to take us over to visit, with his snow machine. We will have to scrunch up tight to fit, but following the roadway, it should be okay. Then I go dig out an old sled I have had for a while, and we get to travel in style, instead. We pack the meat and I stand on the sled runners, Noah rides behind Al and the meat is packed in the sled.

It has been so long since I rode on the runners I figure they will lose me somewhere along the way. But somehow, we make it over in one piece.

Everyone was not expecting anyone to drop in, and some that didn't know us, were not sure they should be welcoming us. The sight of all that meat helped tip the scales in our favor. When we got down to Kara's house, she was very happy to see us.

Shari had been having some pains and was down at Rose's place. They were keeping an eye on her to make sure she was okay. We unloaded the share we brought for Kara and she was happy to have meat to feed the group she was cooking for. She sent some homemade candy she had made home with us. We then went on down to see the rest.

Rose let us in and Shari was feeling better. These were the Braxton Hicks pains she had read about, but still had scared her. Will put their share of meat in the covered back on their little 6 wheeler ATV to keep the ravens and jays out. Rose put hers on her entry porch to freeze up. She gave us some jars of canned diced chicken to vary our diets with and a couple of jars of it for Al, also. She also loaned me some books on goats.

She says she has never raised goats either, although they had goats, just not tame ones. The ones they had were not milk goats, just roamed the hills around their place keeping the brush down. They did raise any that were orphaned and had a hard time keeping them in any pen or fence.

Al is looking fidgety, maybe overload of people around so we say our goodbyes and head for home. This has been so nice, getting to visit and sharing what we have. Rose has a frozen turkey in her old freezer on the porch, that she will prepare at Thanksgiving as a surprise for everyone and probably the last one ever available in our area and we are invited. She thinks maybe it would be good for us all to try to be together once in a while and celebrate the fact that we are alive.

The snow keeps up, not a lot at any one time, just steady off and on. It is accumulating but slowly. So we keep shoveling and clearing larger areas of the yard.

Before the ground freezes too much, I dig out some gravel to keep in the chicken house for them. I know they need it for digestion in their gizzards. I guess I will be keeping all of them over the winter and I think I have enough feed for that. I will let all the hens set that want to, in the spring and raise as many as possible to share with everyone wanting to have some chickens. Eventually I will manage to have enough we can have a chicken dinner. But at present, I think fresh eggs will be the best part. My pullets are starting to lay now and I am getting a few eggs every day. I am saving them back and will share when we go to Rose's for Thanksgiving. Most Bush households are used to buying the 5 dozen egg packs when they grocery shop and most households keep a can or 2 of the powdered eggs on the pantry shelves for the in between shopping trip times. However, powdered eggs just are not a good choice for deviled eggs. By Thanksgiving time, most folks will be dipping into powdered eggs for any eggs used.

Chapter 27

By the end of October, we all realize winter has really come to stay. I just hope we have an early spring to offset it. Everyone out here is hunkered in and keeping busy doing the usual things done all winter anyway. I guess something like the whole world pretty much ending, won't really affect us much until spring. The shock is there, but not really sinking in for us. Once everyone is out of fuel and some food items, then it will start hitting and sinking in.

If it had been spring or summer and easy for the town folk to just hike out here, it would have been much different. Now, it is delayed a bit and maybe soaking in a small amount at a time. No internet, no radio except short wave and few of those left to listen to, also. We have to remember to be alert to anyone showing up with the intent to take what we have, but so far, nothing has happened like that. I am afraid we will become too complacent and be sorry later.

I start setting a trapline starting from the hill across a small gully from my place. I keep checking the snares around the old gut pile, but the ravens, jays and small animals have really been working on it. I only have a few traps and snares, so make a very small trapline I can check often.

I have limited success and move my line a bit farther north. I want to keep as many animals around as possible for the future, also. Pal is nice and helpful in harness, dragging my small sled when we do the trapline. I snowshoe the trails, he pulls along behind me. I carry my rifle when I go, in case I need it. I have a piece of duct tape over the barrel and one on the stock to replace it with if I have to fire it. The tape keeps snow and debris out of the barrel. Traveling on snowshoes is a good way to fall often and it is best to not have to clean the gun after each fall before being able to use it. Even snow coming off branches overhead can clog a barrel, besides going down the back of an unsuspecting neck.

Noah comes along sometimes so he can learn how to trap and how to take care of the animals once they are harvested. On days it has snowed quite a bit, he is handy breaking trails.   We have both gotten much better on the snowshoes and now will be able to hike over to see Rose and Kara any time we want to.   We are doing quite well at keeping the house fire banked enough to be gone several hours without the house freezing up.

In the evenings, we skin and stretch the hides and then work on softening and tanning the hides from previous day's work.

Soon, we have enough to start making some hats, mitts and the baby bunting I want to make for Shari. So I start out by laying out skins and drawing on the skin side with a piece of charred wood from the stove. Once I have the pattern the way I want it, I hold the hide so I won't cut fur as well as skin and cut out the pieces with a razor knife.   I have a large box of dental floss I use for skin sewing.   It is the best for that.   The needles I have are hide sewing needles, with 3 sides at the point, so they slice through the leather.

The bunting goes together quite fast and I use some tanned strips of leather I have to make the ties to fasten it together.   We plan on taking it over in the next few days sometime, if the weather holds around zero and not snowing hard.

When we get around the next day, it is fairly clear and no wind, so we decide just to do it today.   We hurry through caring for the animals and gear up with the snowshoes.   Pal is so used to the harness and sled pulling, he is standing by the sled as we come out the door.   So we take him also.

The walk over doesn't take very long and we are congratulating ourselves on how great we are doing on the snowshoes. Pal suddenly growls and tries to lunge in front of me. The sled holds him back some and almost knocks me down. A large wolf breaks cover right in front of us, heading straight for Pal. Noah has his handgun out and firing before the wolf has a chance to even touch Pal, but I was afraid he would get bit and grabbed his harness trying to hold him. Pal finally settles down as he sees the wolf is no longer a threat. We load the carcass on the sled and Pal is happy to drag the wolf the rest of the way. I will boil the carcass up for chicken feed, they do not mind where the protein comes from. I do the same with most of the animals we trap. I try to waste nothing. I think by boiling it, maybe the chickens won't get the taste for raw flesh and peck on each other. Also maybe head off any type of disease.

After we get to the driveway to Rose and Kara's, we decide to stop there just in case Will and Shari are there for the baby. It is a good thing we do, as they are. Jeremy is watching their place for them and they are staying at Rose's. Shari is very uncomfortable and totally ready for this to be over with. She is still helping out and even does some hiking up and down the hill to Kara's. She is in very good condition, so it should be an easy birth, I hope.

While we are visiting, she gets up every few minutes and walks around. Rose and I look at each other and she nods. We think Shari's wish is about to be granted. She loves the little bunting and shows me some of the other things she has on hand for the baby. Most are at home, but enough here to see her through a couple of days. I made the bunting big enough it will probably last the whole winter as the baby grows. The outside fur is marten and the inside fur is Arctic hare. The baby should need no other cover except in extreme cold. They can carry B B wherever they go without worrying it will get too cold.

As Shari paces through the kitchen her water breaks. She has not realized she is in labor. She cleans herself up and apologizes for the mess as we mop. We are laughing by now and tell her soon she will see what the Bubble Bump actually is, or B B as we have been calling it. She continues pacing, after the contraction is over. This is the best thing she can do, so we all walk with her and talk. We tell jokes and keep her laughing which really isn't too good in a contraction, so we have to pay attention. Rose has a bed set up in the office that used to be her Mom's room. Everything else is cleared out and it has a bed and a chair in the room. She used a filing cabinet as a small dresser so it wouldn't take up much space but give Shari a place to keep clothes.

For a first baby, this one seems to be in a hurry. Shari finally decides she has walked as much as she can, so we let Will help her into bed and prepare her for giving birth. They have a pad on the bed to make it easier to clean up later. There is a tote set up with a pad and soft blankets in it to place the baby in. Everyone scrubs up very well and puts on long sleeved shirts over whatever they are wearing. Rose has some masks used for painting and we use them over our noses and mouths. We look like a comedy routine for backwoods childbirth. There is water heated on the wood stove, although I never figured why boiling water was always called for, no one scalds anything during a birth.

Soon most of us stay out in the living room. Kara and I talk about how we are going to keep our woodsheds filled, after there is no gas for chainsaws. We all have bowsaws, so it looks like we will start cutting each summer as soon as possible to fill the area emptied over the winter and still try to keep at least 2 years ahead.

It seems like only a short time later, but probably not, to Shari, when we hear the sound only a newborn makes and a soft thud of Will hitting the floor. He lasted longer than I thought he would, when he was already green looking when they went in the bedroom.

Soon, the first cry is joined by a 2rd cry. Oh my, sounds like twins. I should have made 2 buntings. Of course, it only takes a little while to make one and I can use this one as a pattern.

When Rose comes out, she looks almost as bad as Will. No one had expected twins. Shari says they are common in her family and her ex was actually a distant cousin. She had twin siblings also, but only one had survived to adulthood. Then he was killed in Iraq.

The new twins were fraternal, a boy and a girl. I guess that is one way to help repopulate the world, have them in groups. I was never one of those women that ooohed and aaaahed over babies, but these 2 were special babies and they seemed to bring out the latent maternal streak I never knew I had. Shari was tired but in good spirits and happy when we finally started home.

We were away a bit longer than I planned when we

left that morning. I was certainly glad the weather was not very cold, only around zero. When we get home, the houses are both cool but not cold, so it doesn't take long to have the fires going again, warming them up. The wolf is brought in to thaw and skin. Noah offers to do that while I cut out another bunting. It is very late by the time I have it done. Noah was already gone for the night, to the cabin. He had his meals with me and helped out around the place during the days, but nights he stayed over there. He only built a fire in the evening to take the main cold off the cabin and let it die out during the night. He didn't want to cut into my stock of firewood too much. We had enough for 2 houses for the winter, but did not want to use it all. Whenever he went along on the trapline, he picked up dead wood along the way and loaded the sled Pal pulled.

The puppies from the dog Roman and Thad brought out were big enough now to start simple training and Noah wanted to get 2 of them. He thought they and Pal could be a small working team and be a big help on hauling things. So 2 days later when we went back over to deliver the new bunting, we brought home 2 rowdy puppies. Pal was not amused. He did a good job teaching them not to chase the cats, although the cats did a fair bit of training on their own. He also let them know outdoors was for the bathroom. I think he housebroke them himself. I made very small harnesses out of scrap rope pieces and when he was harnessed up, they also were harnessed up. At first, they ran along beside him and wanted to play. He nipped them into staying behind him. I started

tying them to each side of the sled, so they would stay
back and soon they thought of it as play and trotted
along nicely or walked along depending on what Pal
was doing. They even learned Gee and Haw and Stop.
I baked some dog treats and would give them and Pal a
treat each time the pups did well. I think bribery is
underrated.

The first trip we made over to Rose's with the 2
pups in their harnesses, everyone was surprised and
amazed we had trained them so well so quickly.
However, Pal was the real trainer of pups. When the
rest of the puppies came tumbling out to see them, Pal
soon set them straight, and they all sat very quietly
around our team. Roman and Thad decided they
wanted to train the ones they had left and see if the
mother was used to a harness, also. She looked like a
sled dog should. Rose had some old harnesses she
had picked up at the Transfer Station several years ago,
so the guys decided to try it out. They went down and
got the harnesses and found one that fit the female.
She stood still to be harnessed so they knew she was
familiar with it. Rose also had some skis under the
shop building that she had picked up, the same way.
She said anyone wanting to try skijoring could give
them a try if they figured out a way to fasten the skis as
they had no bindings on them.

We needed to make some harnesses and tug lines if
we wanted to learn how to run dogs. I guess this
would give us all something to learn and do in winters
now. That would be the time of year that it is easiest
to travel in Alaska. No bugs and the ground is solid
and so is the water. Well, unless there is overflow or a

current under the snow on ice making an open lead.

If we started using dogs, we would need to also start making sleds. I know some of the sled makers use the small black spruce found only in permafrost areas for the frames as they are so fine grained they are extremely strong and flexible when crafted. I think the caribou skin from the caribou Al gave us, will need to be tanned and made into harnesses. The lower legs can be made into boots, and maybe I should see about making boots from the lower legs of the last 2 bears we got, also. I will have to keep boots in mind each time we are skinning, now, so we can shape the hides right and not have to do so much sewing.

Will and Shari were ready to go home with the twins. They were so happy to have 2 buntings now, Shari cried a bit and laughed, saying she was so happy. They were still using the little 6 wheel ATV and bundled babies and Shari in it so they were like a cocoon. After they left, we headed back home, also.

Roman and Thad loaded up our sled with some of the cans of food they stocked up on during the summer. They said that was Noah's, anyway and since he was eating at my place, it would help on food supplies. They didn't want to overload our little team, so let me know there was also a couple bags of rice here for us, and more flour and sugar. I was surprised but it would be nice having even more supplies on hand.

I think this stuff should be stored in the cabin Noah is staying in. If there were ever a house fire, I would like to know we had supplies somewhere else to depend on, and maybe some in the ice house. I still had several empty totes and a few barrels with lids we could store food in and keep rodents and larger animals out. When I talk it over with Noah, he agrees, so when we get home we start filling totes and barrels in the ice house first and a few items in the cabin.

Most of the cans are freeze dried storage foods, so they were very light and there was a lot of them. I was surprised how many they sent over and our tiny team pulled so well. Noah was in the habit of using a large backpack every time we left the house, with some survival gear in it in case we got caught out in bad weather. He now pulled out a small box of chocolate candy. He placed it in my hands and said, "You know I love you, don't you?"

Now that was a surprise, the candy as well as the declaration. I knew we got along very well and he made my insides mush every time he looked at me, but love? Well, yeah, when he wasn't in a room, it felt empty and I looked forward to seeing him every day. We worked well together and neither of us treated the other as anything but a partner in our jobs and chores. The thought of not having him around hurt to think about, so I think that probably means I love him too. I am still staring at the box of chocolates in my hands and he is probably thinking I am really strange. I look up into his eyes and he has the most loving look in his eyes that I have ever seen in my life. Oh those eyes. They have been my downfall from the first day I met him.

Still looking into his eyes, I slowly reach up and give him a soft kiss. The next instant, I am in a bear hug and the breath almost out of me from the steel bands around me as he is kissing me. He suddenly steps back and even maybe blushes a little bit.

"I better not do that or we won't be stopping any time soon," he says and heads on out the door to the little cabin.

Well, this has certainly been quite a day. I set the box of chocolates on the table and stoke the fire. I think I will go to bed a bit earlier this evening and maybe do a lot of thinking.

I have never considered getting married again. The first time was enough to sour a person on that institution for life. However, right now, if Noah asked me, I would say 'Yes' in a heartbeat. What an idea. Who would perform the ceremony and where would it be registered? Does he want a family or will the pets be enough family for us? Wow, he hasn't asked and I am already planning a future together. So much for going to bed early. Now the thoughts going through my head are making it impossible to sleep.

After tossing and turning a while, I get up and light a small propane light. I pull out some of the furs we have tanned and start a Trapper hat. I am not sure who it will be for, so add a piece of elastic in back so it can fit anyone. This is from the first fox caught on the old gut pile. I use some of the leather I had on hand and lined it with Arctic hare fur. Hmmm, maybe I should make some to use as Christmas gifts this year.

Pretty soon there is a small tap at the door. Pal isn't growling, so I open the door. It is Noah. He comes in and sits down across from me.

"Can't sleep either? I am sorry if I am the reason and I hope I didn't mess up our relationship by speaking too soon," he said.

"Well, it was a surprise but a most pleasant one. I have had some thoughts on the subject for a while, but didn't have a clue you did, also."

A slow smile spreads across his face as he leans toward me. "Really? You really have? You sure fooled me."

We sit and talk for an hour or so, then he lightly kisses me on the forehead and heads back out the door. I again stoke up the fire and go to bed. This time, I fall asleep almost as soon as I hit the pillow. We have decided nothing, and didn't even talk about where we were heading. But it feels okay and it feels right. We will take one day at a time and see where it leads.

I was afraid we would be awkward with each other, the next morning, but no, it was more relaxed and felt like we had known each other forever. Our days fell into routine and we enjoyed each other's company very much. We managed to work through any problem that arose without any yelling, name calling or sarcasm.

As Thanksgiving Day approached, we decided on what we would contribute to the dinner being planned over on Rose's place. The actual dinner would be at Kara's as her house was set up better to serve and eat dinner for large groups.

I had a supply of dried sweet potatoes and would make a casserole to take. Also some rolls and maybe a pie or two. Depending on what we could put on the sled easily to pull over without mashing or spilling. We packed some of the fresh eggs in a container so if any broke, they wouldn't mess up the backpack, and Noah would carry them over.

Chapter 28

The weather cooperated and Thanksgiving Day dawned midmorning a bit cloudy but above zero, barely. Not a bad day for a hike. We prepared the load on the sled and headed over to Kara's.

The house was toasty warm when we walked in and eager hands accepted the containers of food we carried. The eggs were an instant hit and Kara started some boiling to make deviled eggs for dinner. We would each get one, but it would be a treat. She said she had some, but they were getting old enough to not do well boiled or any other way, although she was still using them but breaking each one into a cup first, to see if it was able to be used. I told her I would try to get some to her for Christmas dinner, also. Next summer, if all went well, we would try to have a small flock of chickens at each place for eggs and later, some meat.

Will and Shari came with the twins, Dallas and Savannah. The babies had grown quite a bit, but fit in their buntings very well. Since I did not put sleeves on them, they were more of a hooded bag to hold the baby's body heat in. Later, they could be opened down the front and used as a hooded cape.

I met all of Kara's grown children and "adopted" grown children. She always took in strays when they lived in town and the kids needed a place to stay. So all grew up calling her Mom. They still knew the rules and limits at her house and it was fun seeing them all interact. Her grandchildren were so polite and nice, even being the only small children in a sea of adults, they behaved very well. She said that was because when they were little and cute, she didn't let them get away with anything she wouldn't still think was cute when they were 16. It worked very well. There was definite tension between the 2 girlfriends her oldest son brought out when he came. I only hoped that would work itself out well. Both were very nice young women that got in and helped and made themselves useful. One started helping Shari with the babies. She was actually pretty good with them and by the end of the day, they made a deal for her to move over and help Shari. Sounded like a good idea to me. Jeremy came with Will and Shari and was very quiet and subdued in the background, but everyone kept including him in the conversations and asking his opinion until finally he relaxed and enjoyed the day, also.

Rose brought up some bottles of soda that they usually made punch out of for holidays. Everyone was so surprised to find that dinner was a totally traditional Thanksgiving meal that these folks usually did every year. Rose confided that if they had turkey in the future, it would be some she had canned over the years. Not the same, but it would be welcome. She had saved the large bear ham and would bake it for Christmas dinner. We were invited if the weather was okay for travel.

As we were preparing to eat, we heard a snow machine pulling up and everyone went on alert. More guns materialized in hands than I realized were in the room. It was Al, and he had almost a whole moose on his sled behind the snow machine. He wondered if we could use part of it and if he came back and helped, would we show him some more sausage recipes and canning recipes so he could vary his diet a bit more.

Rose and I both said he was welcome to come learn any time and he should come in right now and have dinner with us. He accepted and his eyes bulged at the variety of foods spread out on the serving nook and counters. As we ate, he told us how he got the moose on the sled. It had somehow managed to get its head through one of his wolf snares and strangled itself just before he got there. It was still warm, so he hurried and butchered it up. Then on his way by his cabin, he unloaded a couple of chunks to use fresh and brought the rest over to share. He dropped the hide off at my place, since he seen me working on the caribou hides he left last time. After dinner, he took a shoulder down for Rose to butcher out for fresh meat for the group there and we all headed back to my place to store the rest and he would come by tomorrow so we could start on the meat. This had truly been a Thanksgiving that had much to be thankful for.

I showed him how to cut the leg skins next time to make himself a pair of boots from the hind legs with very little sewing. He was surprised and said he would do that on any more he got.

I trimmed a bit off the meat, sliced very thin, and marinated it a while in some spices, then drained and set to dry on the rack I had over my heater stove. Before I went to bed, I turned the strips and they were getting firm. By morning, they were still chewy but could be considered jerky.

Noah and I started immediately on cutting up the meat. Al showed up a bit later and we asked how much he wanted as sausage. Then he tried a strip of the jerky. "Okay, you made this just overnight? I would really like some of the meat fixed this way, for trail food." he said.

So we set some of the muscle pieces out on the porch to partially freeze and then brought it in and sliced very thin. I started more marinating in some stainless steel bowls I have, and we continued cutting meat and deciding what to do with it.

I made some chicken fried steaks from some loin

and we ate them on warm rolls from the oven. We stopped work on the meat in late afternoon. Al went home and we took care of the animals again. The goats enjoyed a bit of being out and running around in the pens. The chickens, not so much. I only let them out a little bit at a time so they didn't freeze their combs or feet. That gave me a chance to clean their coop and keep it from smelling too bad in there.

When Al came back the next day, he came by dog power on cross country skis. He said it wasn't as fast, but almost and saved gas. Besides, if he kept eating here, he was going to be fat soon and didn't want that to happen. As I looked at his lean rangy body, I didn't think there was ever any danger of him getting fat. The work done here indoors and out, does not support getting very overweight.

The batch of jerky I dried overnight was moved from over the stove and a new batch put on the racks. Al figured he should build himself some racks and he could take a bunch of the meat home and dry it himself. Since he had a lot of the caribou sausage left and it was too cold to smoke any more, he decided he would go ahead and take what he wanted of the meat home, and make jerky, now that he knew how. So we loaded up his backpack with the boned out meat and he and his dog headed for home.

I knew Kara only liked game meat as jerky and hot spicy jerky at that, so made a large batch of extremely spicy jerky to give her for Christmas. I made some teriyaki jerky and some brown sugar jerky with only a hint of spice on it.

The next several days was spent making jerky and

the usual chores around the place. The hay cut during the summer was holding up very well. We had not fed out as much as I thought we would by now, so may even have some left over in the spring.

The Trapper hats I was making were coming along very well, also. I still had the wolf hides that I was working soft. I used the face pieces as mitt backs from the 2 we got around the old gut pile. The palms were made out of some leather I had on hand and I lined them with a fleece mitt and an Arctic hare inner liner. Both liners could be removed to replace or dry. I braided some leather thongs together and made a mitt harness to wear over the head so the mitts would hang handy if a person had to pull their hands out to work or do something the mitts were too clumsy for.

The big old wolf Noah shot between here and Rose's, I softened and cut in wide bands for parka hood ruffs. I didn't have enough materials to make whole parkas, but I did have enough to make hoods with the ruffs around them and a short cape to place over upper back and chest. Then a coat put on over would make it complete and give extra warmth where it is usually needed. Each one was a different color fabric on the outside, so they would be easy to tell apart. From the scraps, I made some small hoods for the twins. From a couple of strips, I made toy ice worms. I sewed some eyes at one end of each strip and these would be for the babies later and for the youngest child over at Kara's. I decided to give the older boy one of my knives in a holster I made for it. Every boy needed his own knife and although he may already have one, another is fine, also.

Noah wanted to make something special for his Dad and brother, so we made boots out of the hind feet of the 2 bears we got in the autumn. These boots would leave very odd tracks and we decided the grizzly would be for Roman, the black bear for Thad. Noah did the heavy sewing and I made some liners and inner soles to wear in them. Noah used some of the leather thongs to make wrap ties around the ankles and up the calves to hold the boots on.

We went out and found a small scraggly cartoon tree and brought it in and decorated it for our presents to go under. The ones we were to take over to Kara and Rose, we wrapped in old newspaper and labeled. We had a pretty good stack going there and the cats thought it was fun to run up and down the pile, knocking packages every direction. I was smart enough not to add the packages of jerky, yet.

Early on Christmas morning, we loaded up the sled and hooked up Pal and his 2 minions. I dumped extra feed in for the goats and the chickens and we were off. The dogs were in fine spirits and it was not a cold day, with no wind. We arrived in time to hand out presents. At Roman and Thad's, they were so surprised with their gifts and had to put them on, immediately which set the pups into a frenzy, first trying to get to them, then trying to get away from them. Hmmm, maybe we didn't get all the smell of bear out of them. They handed us packages as we stepped out to continue on down the hill.

Next stop was Kara's and she was fixing breakfast for the bunch she fed every day. We had breakfast and handed out packages there and then on down to Rose's.

She was pleased with her hood and jerky and handed us a couple of packages to take home with us. We would open ours after we returned home.

Next we went on down to Will and Shari's. They were very surprised to see us here. Shari loved the things I made for the babies and the hood for her. Ashley liked hers, also. Will and Jeremy were very pleased with the Trapper hats. The jerky we gave as being from us and from Al. They handed us a couple of packages to add to our growing pile and we headed back toward our place. As we got to the driveway, we met Al, just coming from his place, so we all went on in to the house. The dogs were happy with the large bones I had saved from the butchering earlier, of the caribou then marinated and smoked a bit for them, so they had flavor. They performed very well today and deserved a treat. I gave Al's dog one also so he wouldn't feel left out. We hauled our packages in and placed them under the tree with ours to each other. Al brought in a package and added it, too. We gave him the packages we had for him and he was surprised to find a new Trapper hat and mitts. The wolf head mitts I gave to Noah. The marten Trapper hat was for him, also. Al asked about learning to fur sew sometime in the future and I said okay, any time. Noah told him about the bear feet boots he made for his Dad and brother. Al thought he had some bear skins around and would look them over, so I told him to cut any he got in future with boots in mind and it would save a lot more sewing the same as with moose and caribou. Just cutting in different places. These won't be good boots for anything but winter.

Al doesn't stay and we finally open the rest of our presents. Everything is something we can use or eat. Almost everything is homemade. Rose made us each a vest with lots of pockets to carry gear when we are out working. Mine has items in some of the pockets to help out on different jobs. Kara gave us both homemade candy and cookies and a crocheted beanie type hat each. The guys gave us some different types of dried canned foods to add variety to our diet.

We fix dinner together and talk over what a pleasant day it has been. We have been truly blessed.

As we relax that evening, Noah reaches in his pocket and hands me a very small package. It is a ring. He made it himself and says, "I don't want you to think I am pushing a bit here, but I would like you to know I love you and plan on us having a future together. I am not asking right now, I am just wanting you to be thinking about it."

As if I would be thinking of much of anything else. The thought of not having him here is painful. I look forward to seeing him each morning and feel like part of me has left when he leaves in the evening. I think he may be the best thing to happen to me in a long time. I turn to him and say, "I love you too."

He sits there stunned for half a moment then grabs me in a bear hug and just holds me close.

"I don't know how or when, but I want to marry you," he whispers in my ear. Then he goes over to his cabin for the night.

Wow, okay, I was expecting him to say something, but that was way off in the future. It's too soon to be the future.

I want to talk to someone else about it, and the next morning, suggest we go back over and visit at Rose's. He can spend some time with his Dad and I will go talk to Rose. The weather is holding steady and we may not get another chance for quite a while. He agrees, so we harness up the little team and head out.

When we get to the main road, we go north to check the snares at the old gut pile and are surprised to find 2 wolves. We take them out of the snares and reset. Then we drop the wolves off in our driveway and go on south to Rose's.

Noah stays up at his Dad's and I go on down the hill to see Rose. She is surprised to see me and invites me in. I get right to the point and tell her there is a good possibility we will be getting married if we can figure out how to do it now. She tells me she is able to perform weddings legally and so can Kara, Paul and Samantha. I don't understand until she tells me they are registered as ministers. She does not know how legal it would be since right now, there is no legal system anywhere, as much as we can tell. She says we can always start a registry and write in all the data. Keep it just to record births, deaths and marriages. Maybe property transactions also, in future.

We design a page to use for a license and print several out on her laptop. She says she should do a lot of the assorted papers they may need in future because she don't know how long her battery system or ink cartridges are going to hold out. So while we are at it, we try to figure out what may be needed in the next several years and make several copies of each form. I take one with me when I leave to go home. I stop and say Hi to Kara on my way by, then on up to Roman's. The guys are out working with the puppies and Pal looks very disgruntled. He is training puppies to be good little sled dogs. Our 2 are actually a big help. With Pal in front and our 2 pups behind, the ones in the middle almost have to go where they are supposed to. They get nipped from the rear if they pull back and growled at from the front if they don't stay in place.

They end the lesson and we head for home. We pick up the wolves as we go through the driveway. We will have to thaw to skin them.

The fire is very low when we get in the house, so I fill it up and let it burn a bit to make sure it is going well. The house isn't cold, but it isn't really too warm, either. I think the temperature has dropped since we left this morning. When I check the thermometer, I see that it is now -15 degrees F. When I check an hour later, it is -20. Yes, we may be starting another cold spell. Noah brings in firewood while I start dinner.

Over dinner, I tell him what Rose has told me. His face lights up and he comes around the table and kisses me. "You have been thinking about it too? Can we really do this? I would love to spend the rest of my life with you." He tells me he wanted to propose the first day he met me. Wow, that would have sent me running. Probably for a gun.

Chapter 29

The temperature keeps dropping and by the next afternoon, it is -40. We have the wood stove going in the barn for the goats. It won't keep the whole building as warm as the house, but we just want to keep it above zero or so., so the goats don't suffer. We keep water on the stove also to give them liquid water to drink at least twice a day.

I have the windows open from the house to the sun porch to keep the chicken coop a bit warmer than usual. The vent holes in the walls between the house and the coop are also all wide open. The chickens

aren't dumb and are staying up near the vents.   There
is only 1 or 2 eggs a day now and they roll down the
chute from the nest boxes onto a tray on the sun
porch.   The transplanted lettuce is still producing but
growing very slowly at these temperatures and I still
have a few tomatoes ripening on the sad looking plants.
I sprout a few seeds to add to the lettuce and onion
pickings and a few celery leaves once in a while for a
small salad each for us.   I give the chickens some of
the sprouts now and then, also.

I will try to enlarge my winter growing area on the
sun porch this coming summer.   It will be worth it.
Rose does the same thing on her porch and shares with
Kara.

When Noah goes out to check on the goats, I hear a
shot.   Then Noah is bursting through the door and he
is ashen faced and collapses on the floor.   I have my
handgun out in my hand but still seated on the couch
when another figure bursts through the door.   He is
bundled in furs but I can see the white on his face that
means frostbite and it looks like he has a bad case of it.
As I look closer, I see it is Royal.   Of all the people to
survive the quake and weather in Fairbanks, why did it
have to be him?   Somehow he missed Will and Shari's
place on his way by and stumbled into mine, instead.
But Noah is hit.   As I start to bend down to check,
Royal waves his gun at me and tells me to stay still or
join him.   I ask him why he is doing this and why did
he act as though his sons were still alive.   Wrong thing
to say.   He goes into screaming mode and waving the
gun around.   In his rambling diatribe, he confesses to
having rigged the accident that killed Shari's parents so

his son could have their money. Then they couldn't find Shari to arrange an accident for her. But since they found her in the wilds of Alaska, they figured she could disappear and be presumed dead in short order. Maybe after wild animals had chewed her up enough to not show how she died.

While he is yelling, I see Noah open his eyes and look at me. At least he is still alive. As Royal goes on about what an ungrateful wife she was, I slowly raise my handgun beside my leg. Somehow he and his buddies had learned that Shari had been staying here after Rod and Rob were killed. In his mind, he thought she and I were in on it together. So I was going to have to pay. By this time the warmth of the house was starting to thaw his flesh and he was clawing at his face trying to get the pain to stop. His breathing is raspy also, as though he had frosted his lungs a bit. He was so intent on revenge that he didn't cover his face and breathe through the fur.

As I am about to put him out of his misery, the door swings open yet again and Jeremy slides in behind Royal. He grabs him by some pressure point in his neck and Royal drops like a stone. As Royal goes down, I am on my knees beside Noah. I ask if he can talk and he says yes, he can, he is just nicked, he thinks.

By this time, Jeremy has Royal trussed up and unarmed. He offers to set him outside so we don't have to look at him, but I just can't bring myself to let him freeze that way. I was willing to shoot him earlier but this seems a bit cold blooded. Jeremy shrugs and says he knows it is cruel, but look at the man. He is so frozen already he will lose his face and probably parts of feet and hands, maybe other parts we can't see and don't want to see. It may be kinder to let him never regain consciousness. I guess he has a point there.

We pull off Noahs parka and shirt to see that he really was only nicked but not a good looking nick. The flesh was swollen around it on his side over his ribs. I took his fur parka outdoors and rubbed snow in the blood on the fur. It froze and came off pretty well. I hung the parka out on the entryway porch to air some. I would shake it out more later to get any other blood off it, I hoped.

Jeremy had Noah patched up pretty well when I went back in. He had recognized Royal as he skied by. Royal had not seen him. So he followed along a bit behind, trying to figure out what Royal was going to do. He was sorry he didn't get here in time to stop Noah from getting shot.

Royal was coming around by then, so Jeremy said he would take him along with him unless we wanted to keep him. I certainly didn't and neither did Noah. So the 2 men left. Royal was still screaming at Jeremy as they went out the door. I don't think I want to know what is going to happen next.

Noah is still a little woozy from the shock of being shot. So he stretches out on the couch. I cover him with a large quilt I have handy and he dozes off to sleep.

When he wakes up a bit later, he is flushed and doesn't look or feel too good. I take the bandage off his side and it does not look good. I sponge him off and give him some aspirin to lower his fever. I find some of my homemade medicines and also some

essential oils. The oils should help get rid of infection.
I have him turn so I can drop the oil directly on the
wound. I place peppermint oil directly on it, then
thieves oil around it and then on it. After a bit, the
redness and swelling go down, around the furrow on
his side. I fix some hot tea for him and sweeten it a
bit and he sips it. His color is getting better, so I help
him get comfortable and he dozes back off to sleep. I
gear up and go check on the goats. They are doing
fine and I stoke up their stove in there, then close it
down enough to keep burning but not too much. The
barn feels pretty good compared to outdoors. The
goats seem content so I close up and latch all the doors
and window shutters.

    I grab an armload of firewood as I go back to the
house. Make each trip out in this count. I feed the
chickens and give them fresh water.

    When I am done with the animal chores, I start a
pot of soup going on the stove. It will be easier for
Noah to sip some if he continues not feeling very well
or even if he feels fine.

    Noah wakes up as the soup is ready and he looks
much better. I put more oils on his side and he barely
flinches as I rub it around the wound. He tells me he
probably would not have been shot except he didn't
want to let Royal come in with no warning. He also
didn't want to turn his back on him to come in ahead
of him. Royal got the jump on him as he came out of
the barn and was fastening the door. He certainly had
to start paying more attention to what was around,
even in these temperatures. This was no longer our
comfortable old life. Even one slip up could be the

end for any one of us.

As he sips his mug of soup, he looks at me oddly and then says "You were just going to shoot him, weren't you?"

"Well, yeah, I wasn't going to let him do any more damage to the man I love.   Bad enough he hurt you at all."   Then I kissed him on the forehead.

He grabbed my hand and tugged me closer.   So I kissed him on the mouth.   Much better.

Chapter 30

Well, it is the end of the old year and what a year it has been. The world has come to an end, as we knew it. As far as I can tell, there will be no commerce or government as such, any time in the foreseeable future. Whatever supplies we have on hand in anything, is going to have to last, and last, and last. There will be no running to the store if something runs out. We are going to have to find alternatives for just about everything. If not for ourselves, then for our children and grandchildren.

In some ways, the future looks grim, in others, maybe the best that could have happened to us.

There has been murder, there has been new lives

enter our sphere. There will be more in the future. It is human nature.

I am going to get married sometime in the spring. That is if we can wait until spring.

Some recipes used in the story, from my cookbook, "Don't Use A Chainsaw In The Kitchen"

LAUNDRY SOAP
1 bar grated Fels Naptha soap, Heat on the stove in a large pot of water until melted. (About 1 gal of water)
1 C. Washing Soda,
1 C. Borax
  Add the hot Fels mixture to a 5 gal bucket, mix in the soda and borax, fill about 3/4 full with hot water. Cover the bucket with a lid and store it in a cool dry place. It gels. Keep a small plastic bucket full where you do laundry and use a 1/2 Cup dipper to measure into the washing machine. It doesn't foam up like detergent, but does a good job cleaning clothes.

HONEY CINNAMON BREAD
Put 2 cups of warm water in a large bowl. Add ¼ cup honey, 1 t. salt and 2 T. oil or melted butter. Add 2 cups of flour and a pack or 2 T. dry yeast. Beat at

least 50 strokes.   Batter should sheet off the spoon.
Add 2 more cups of flour and stir, then knead in.
May add a bit more flour if dough is too sticky to
handle, but it should be soft.   Grease bowl and turn
dough so all sides are greased.   Cover and let rise until
double.   Punch down.   May do this twice for a finer
grained bread.   After dough has finished rising and
been punched down for the last time, turn out onto a
lightly floured surface and gently knead to make sure
all air pockets are out.   Roll dough out so it is the
length of the bread pan on one side.   Sprinkle
powdered honey or spread liquid honey on dough,
sprinkle cinnamon to taste over the honey.   Roll up the
dough, tuck in the ends and place seam side down in
the greased pan to rise again.   Brush the top with oil
and allow to rise until almost double, then bake in 375
degree F. oven for 15 minutes, then turn oven down to
350 degrees F. to finish.   Loaf should sound hollow
when thumped and be starting to pull away from the
sides of the pan.   Cool on rack.

To test for how much bread has risen, poke the dough
lightly with your finger.   If the dent remains or only
slowly comes back up, dough has risen enough.   It
dent pops right back out, let the dough raise longer.
If the whole works collapses, it has risen too long.
Knead well and shape and watch closer for it to be
ready to bake.

SOURDOUGH BREAD

Night before, add 2½ cups flour, 2 cups warm water to
Starter.   Next day.   Save 1 cup for Starter.   Dissolve 1
package yeast in 2 cups liquid, (potato water, water,

milk, whatever) add ¼ cup margarine, oil or shortening, ¼ cup honey or sugar. Add sourdough and 2 cups flour, stir until well mixed. Beat 50 strokes to develop gluten. Blend 2 T. sugar, 2 t. salt, 2 t. soda until no lumps, sprinkle over top of dough and stir in gently. Cover, let rise ½ hour. Stir down and add 4 cups flour, turn out and knead well. Shape, place in greased pans, pans should be half full, let rise until double. Bake at 400 degree oven for 20 minutes, turn down to 325 degrees, bake until it starts to pull away from the pans. Turn out on racks to cool. Butter loaves if you like a soft crust, brush with water if you like crusty loaves, as soon as loaves are placed on rack.

An easy starter is simply to mix 1 cup flour, 1 cup warm water and 1 teaspoon yeast together. Let set 24 hours in a warm spot in the house. It should develop a pleasantly sour odor, similar to buttermilk. Always use a container large enough for expansion. Sometimes sourdough will go to great lengths to run over the sides of its container. Glass or plastic and a loose fitting lid. Or graniteware.

ENGLISH MUFFINS (Do not require an oven)
    In a large bowl, mix 2 cups flour, 2 T. sugar or honey, 2 t. salt and 1 T or envelope of dry yeast. Set aside. In pan, heat 1 ¾ cup milk, ¼ cup water and 1 T. butter or margarine until very warm (120 to 130 degrees). Add gradually to flour mixture and beat at least 150 strokes. Add 1 egg and 1 cup flour. Beat as fast as you can for another 150 strokes. Add enough

flour to make a soft dough. Knead until smooth and elastic, adding more flour if dough is sticky. Cover with plastic wrap and let rise in a warm place until double, about 1 hour. Punch down, cover and let rise another 45 minutes, punch down again. Roll out to ½ inch thick. Cut with 3 ¼ inch round cutter or clean tuna can with both ends removed. Sprinkle cookie sheets lightly with corn meal, place muffins about an inch apart and sprinkle with additional cornmeal. Cover lightly and let rise until double. Heat lightly greased griddle or heavy skillet. With wide spatula, carefully move muffins to griddle. Do not puncture or compress or muffins will collapse. Cook over very low heat 8 to 10 minutes on each side or until lightly browned. Muffins should sound hollow when tapped. Cool on racks. Makes about 24.

GAME MEAT MARINATED IN BEER
One lean roast, any kind of meat, placed in a large zippered baggie. Add 1 can or bottle of any kind of beer, a dash of garlic and some Italian or other seasonings. Zip bag closed while removing as much air as possible so the beer is in contact with as much meat as possible. Marinate overnight or at least several hours. Carefully remove the meat, saving the marinade. Coat meat in flour and brown in hot oil in a Dutch oven. Place the Dutch oven with the meat and added marinade in a slow oven (300 to 325 degrees F.) after covering tightly with the lid or tin foil. Bake several hours. Meat should be very well done and fork tender. May add sliced carrots, onions and potatoes for the last 2 hours of cooking.

BROWNIE PUDDING
Mix:
3/4 cup sugar,
1 1/4 cup flour,
2 T. cocoa, 2 t. baking powder,
1 t. salt
     Add:
2 T. oil, 1 T. vanilla,
1 cup milk
     Mix well, pour into 9 x 9 pan, then mix:
1 3/4 cup brown sugar, 1/4 cup cocoa, 1½ cup hot water
Pour over cake batter, do not stir, bake at 350 degrees for 40 to 45 minutes. Serve warm.
May add ½ cup chopped nuts to cake batter.
Excellent served with ice cream.

CANNED COLESLAW
1 head shredded cabbage
1/2 c chopped onions
2 cups sugar
2 tsp salt
1 tsp celery seed
1 tsp mustard seed
1/2 scant cup vinegar
optional: shredded green peppers
Mix, let sit 4 hours. Pack into jars, to 1/2 inch of the top. Process in boiling water bath 7 minutes - DO NOT OVER COOK!!
This makes a sweet-sour pickle, served like slaw. You

can drain and add some oil before serving if you want
or creamy salad dressing.   It is good just like it is,
though.

STIR FRY GARLIC RABBIT or CHICKEN
Serve over hot rice
Slice raw chicken breast into thin bite sized pieces, half
frozen slices easiest.   Set aside.   Slice whatever fresh
vegetables you have on hand or like into small uniform
pieces.   I usually use onion, broccoli, celery and bell
peppers, some bok choy is good, also.   Mix 1 T.
cornstarch, 3 T. soy sauce, 2 t. minced garlic in a cup,
add enough water to make almost 1 cup total, set aside.
Heat skillet or wok with very small amount of oil until
hot and add the chicken, stirring to cook quickly, add
the veggies halfway through the chicken being cooked
and just before the vegetables are almost done, stir in
the liquids after stirring well.   Stir and cook until liquid
turns fairly clear and thickens.   May add a few drops
of sesame oil as you remove from heat and stir through
for sesame garlic chicken.

BEER BATTER HALIBUT
½ cup corn starch, ½ cup flour, 3 T. season salt, 2 t.
garlic powder, and an 11 or 12 ounce can or bottle of
beer.   Mix all ingredients together, mixture should be
the consistency of cream.   Add more beer if too thick.
Cut halibut into 1 ounce chunks or long strips, dredge
in flour, then dip in batter.   Deep fry until they float,
or about 3 minutes.
Any mild flavored fish may be substituted for halibut

CAMPFIRE ROAST

One large boneless piece of meat. Pierce deeply with a knife, adding jalapeno peppers, green onions or cloves of garlic here and there over the whole roast. Rub the surface with salt and pepper. Either wrap the whole roast in several layers of aluminum foil, sealing well, and bury under the campfire or fire pit. Add several inches of dirt, pull the coals back over and build up the fire a bit. Allow it to die down for the day while you are hunting. OR, rub flour over the entire surface of the roast and brown in a hot Dutch Oven in a small amount of oil or grease. Cover with a tight fitting lid and cook slowly until done. This can be buried under the campfire also if you are careful not to loosen the lid so dirt gets into it. Serve in the evening after the days' hunt or work, with hot Bread-On-A-Stick that each person cooks over the campfire.

CAJUN ROAST

Large turkey-sized roasting bag, large pan to bake in.
8 or 9 pound rolled roast, or any boneless roast (8 cloves garlic, 8 green onions and
4 green chilies) Save green onion tops to add later. Poke holes in roast and insert cloves of garlic, green onions and chilies. Cut green onions off flush with outside of roast.
Cover roast with salt and crushed red peppers. Place 2 T. flour in roasting bag, shake well, smooth flour on bottom of bag, placed in large pan. Add roast, 2 pounds mushrooms, 8 medium potatoes, 8 carrots, 1

cup chopped green onion tops (from green onions pushed down into roast and tops cut flush with outside of roast), 1/2 cup parsley, 1/2 cup water, I T. celery seed, 2 cups wine, 2 T. soy sauce, 1/2 t angostura bitters. Pour the liquid carefully into the bottom of the bag. Seal bag, Poke holes in top of bag -with a fork. Bake at 325 to 350 degrees until roast reaches required degree of doneness. If you are using game meat for this recipe, you may wish to wait until the last hour of baking to add the vegetables. Most game meat should be cooked well-done. If not using roasting bag, use a good tight fitting roaster pan and lid.

MOCK CHICKEN FRIED STEAKS

To 1 pound of any ground game meat, add 1 raw egg, 2 slices of bread and 1/4 cup milk or water. Mix very well, but not until mushy. May beat egg, bread and liquid well, before adding meat. Form into 1/2 inch thick patties. Coat with flour, dip in milk or water, then into fine bread or cracker crumbs. Allow to set for 5 to 10 minutes, brown in 2 T. hot oil on each side, season with salt, garlic and pepper to taste. Serve with cream gravy.

I usually use a coarsely ground game meat for this recipe. Bear, moose or venison works very well.

SWEDISH SAUSAGE
5 lb pork
5 lb beef
5 lb of veal

5 lb of potatoes
5 large onions
nutmeg 1 to 2 nuts grated,   about 2 Tablespoons
2 tsp all spice
2 tsp cinnamon
salt and pepper to taste
grind all together starting with the coarse grind
working to the smallest grind you have then stuff in
casings.

WTLTED LETTUCE SALAD

Clean and dry 2 large bunches leaf lettuce, tear in bite-
sized pieces into bowl, season lightly with salt and
pepper, add 2 t. sugar and 2 sliced green onions. Fry 4
slices bacon crisp, crumble, set aside. Add 1/4 cup
cider vinegar and 2 T. water to bacon drippings, heat to
boiling,   pour over lettuce. Toss until wilted and evenly
coated. Add crumbled bacon and 2 sliced hardboiled
eggs. Makes about 4 servings.

MOLASSES TAFFY

Butter sides of heavy kettle, add:
1 cup unsulfured molasses
1 cup sugar
1 T. butter or margarine
dash of salt
Cook until mixture reaches 270 degrees, pour onto
greased platter or cookie sheet.   As edges cool, fold
toward center.   When cool enough to handle, press
into ball with buttered fingers.   Pull until light colored
and very firm.   Stretch into long rope ½ inch in

diameter and cut into 1 inch pieces. Wrap each piece in waxed paper or plastic wrap.

SPRUCE TIP JELLY

3 cup spruce tip juice, 4 cups sugar, 1 package pectin

Day One: Prepare the Spruce Tip Juice

1. Rinse 3-4 cups of spruce tips in cold water. Drain and then lightly chop them.
2. Place the spruce tips in a small saucepan with 3 1/2 cups cold water. Bring to a boil and then immediately remove them from the heat.
3. Transfer the tips and liquid to a heatproof bowl, cover tightly, and let steep overnight.

Day Two: Make Your Jelly

1. Sterilize 5 half-pint jars.
2. Collect the spruce tip juice by straining the liquid through a jelly bag, or several layers of cheesecloth. (If you use a jelly bag or cheesecloth, be sure to dunk it in scalding water first — not just to cleanse it, but to hydrate it so a dry cloth doesn't soak up the juice.)
3. Measure 3 cups of spruce tip juice into a 6- or 8-quart saucepot.
4. Measure the sugar into a separate bowl.
5. Stir the entire packet of pectin into the saucepot. (I had heard some great things about MCP pectin. Also, it dissolved nicely, without lumps. If you use a different brand of pectin, be sure to follow the recipe directions in that box. I'd use the proportions given for mint jelly.)
6. Bring the mixture to a full rolling boil, on high heat, stirring constantly.
7. Quickly stir in the sugar. Return the mixture to a rolling boil and boil for exactly 2 minutes, stirring

constantly. Remove from heat and skim foam.

8. Ladle or pour the hot jelly into the sterilized jars, leaving 1/4-inch head space. Wipe the rims with a clean, damp cloth and secure the lids. Process in a water-bath canner, using the correct time for your altitude: 5 minutes for 0-1,000 feet above sea level, plus 1 minute for every additional 1,000 feet.

Yields about 5 half-pint jars. (If you want more than this, plan to make multiple small batches.)

ROSE PETAL VINEGAR

2 cups white wine vinegar (heat to near boil)
1 cup rose petals (white ends removed)
3 or 4 whole cloves

Gently crush the petals to bruise a bit. In a sterilized canning jar, place the rose petals and cloves. Pour hot vinegar over top, roughly mash the petals with a wooden spoon and seal. Set aside for 10 days at room temperature and in the dark. Shake once a day. Strain vinegar and discard the cloves and rose petals.

ROSE PETAL JAM

2 cups rose petals (finely chopped, remove the white part,   bottom of the petal, and discard it.)
2 cups boiling water
2 3/4 cups sugar
3 tablespoons honey
1 tablespoon lemon juice

Cover the rose petals with boiling water, simmer for 10 minutes. Strain and reserve both water and petals. Add sugar and the honey to the water. Simmer for 30 minutes. add lemon and finely chopped petals and simmer 30 minutes. Pour into hot jars.   Water bath 10 minutes.

Baking Tip:

If you are using only whole wheat flour and want your cakes to turn out as though you were using all white bleached flour, exchange one quarter of the measure of flour with corn starch.

Other books by Rosalyn Stowell

The Dark of Night
An Alaskan PAW Novel
Written by Mrs. Rosalyn E. Stowell
The continuing story of Maxie, Noah and their neighbors after the Great Quake.
Book 2   218 pages
R. E.\Stowell
ISBN-13: 978-0615760780 (Custom Universal)
ISBN-10: 0615760783
BISAC: Fiction / Romance / Suspense

The Dawn
An Alaskan PAW Novel
Written by Mrs. Rosalyn E. Stowell
This is book 3 in the continuing saga of Maxie, Noah and their friends and neighbors
Black & White on White paper
216 pages

R. E.\Stowell
ISBN-13: 978-0615769370 (Custom Universal)
ISBN-10: 0615769373
BISAC: Fiction / Action & Adventure

ALASKAN GOLD
Non Illegitimus Carborundum
An Alaskan Novel
Written By Mrs. Rosalyn Stowell

A spur of the moment decision to check out her inheritance in person just might be the best thing to ever happen or maybe not. Why won't ex-fiancés stay ex'd and how do you tell Toads from the Prince's? An ex Fiance' that refuses to admit he is an ex, an Attorney that is not looking for long term, an Environmentalist looking to shut down mining and the boy next door. How to choose?. Set in Alaska, maybe 20 years ago or so, join Jo as she learns about living, loving and mining in the Bush , not always in that order.

My cookbook. Over 30 years in the making.

Don't
Use
A
Chainsaw
In The Kitchen!!

Cabin Etiquette or Harmony in the Bush

1. Always go outside to cut frozen meat, if you are using a chainsaw.
2. If you open it, close it.
3. If you break it, admit it.
4. If you can't fix it, find someone who can, or replace it.
5. If it wasn't given to you or you didn't buy or make it, it's not yours, leave it alone.
6. Always leave some firewood for the next person.
7. If you make a mess, clean it up.
8. If you're sorry, say so.
9. If you kill something, clean it.
10. Leave everything in better condition than you found it.
11. If you value it, take care of it.
12. If you turn it on, turn it off.
13. If you borrow it, return it.
14. If you move it, put it back.
15. If it belongs to someone else, get permission to use it.

Rosalyn Stowell

8.5" x 11" (21.59 x 27.94 cm)
Black & White on White paper
260 pages
R.E.Stowell
ISBN-13: 978-0615724324 (Custom Universal)
ISBN-10: 0615724329
BISAC: Cooking / Methods / Canning & Preserving
Over 400 recipes and assorted how-to directions, on

butchering, making sausage, building a trappers cabin, tanning hides and my autobiography at the back of the book.

About the writer:

I live 40 miles beyond phone or power lines. Over 50 miles beyond mail delivery. No TV, no radio, no door to door salesmen or politicians. Also no running water. It makes life simpler and a lot more fun. Of course, there is also no trash pickup or sidewalks. However, what there is, is a life full of interesting things to do and I have never been bored, ever.

I have lived in Alaska since 1969. I am a widow. I've operated heavy equipment, cooked, been a goldsmith, a taxidermist and a Registered Guide. I've built cabins and houses, waited tables, (very briefly, something to do with a pitcher of ice water and a customer) and peeled logs, painted pictures and worked as an artist's model to buy food and clothes for my children. I've even chauffeured for a while. I have held licenses as Boiler Operator, Taxidermist, Mill Operator, Registered Hunting Guide, Fishing Guide and for Mining. Life is interesting so be prepared for anything. You never know what is going to happen next.

www.ingramcontent.com/pod-product-compliance
Lightning Source LLC
Chambersburg PA
CBHW060630260626
47161CB00008B/2847